To all the readers and writers in
London's East End who were
once thought not to exist,
but clearly do.

Brick Lane Bookshop
Short Story Prize

Longlist 2019

A Brick Lane Bookshop Publication

Design and typesetting by Kate Ellis
Project-managed by Kate Ellis

First published by Brick Lane Bookshop in 2019

ISBN 978-1-9162-0820-9

Brick Lane Bookshop
166 Brick Lane
London
E1 6RU

www.bricklanebookshop.org

Printed and bound in Great Britain by Clays Ltd, Elcograf S.p.A.

Contents

Foreword

Denise Jones

I'm delighted that Brick Lane Bookshop has published this book of twelve short stories out of the 463 entered into our short story competition. We were overwhelmed by the response and extremely impressed by the quality of the entries, so thanks to all the writers who entered their work. I also want to thank Kate Ellis, who organised the competition for the bookshop, Jarred McGinnis and all the first readers, and especially our judges, Emma Paterson, Kit Caless and Zoe Gilbert, who selected the shortlist and 2019 winner.

This competition is a refreshed idea from Brick Lane Bookshop's history when it was known as Eastside Books.

From 1980 I worked with Eastside Wordcentre, a charity supported by the Arts Council, at 178 Whitechapel Road. This was a centre for the spoken word in east London, running Eastside Books and a host of groups and workshops aimed at encouraging writing. The writing-development programme consisted of residencies in local schools, writers' workshops, short courses, small publications and a newsletter on literature in east London. We worked with a culturally diverse population, assisting people in practical ways to take pleasure in reading and writing, and demystifying the world of publishing. We were members of the Federation of Worker Writers and Community Publishers (FWWCP), a national federation of bookshops and writers' groups that supported new and working-class writers.

In 1994, literature development workers Mandy Berry, Roger Mills and Ruby Dawson and I launched the Eastside Wordcentre's first Eastside Stories Novel Bursary, for writers living in the east London boroughs of Tower Hamlets, Hackney and Newham who were working on their first novel. There was a cash prize sponsored by Texaco and, for the winner, an introduction to Darley Anderson, a leading literary agent.

Applicants were required to submit a synopsis of their novel with an extract of 5,000 words. We received entries from a range of writers, with different ages, experience and styles of writing. Some had been trying to get published for years, while for others it was a first attempt at writing a novel.

Ben Richards was the first winner with his entry *Throwing the House out of the Window*, which was later published by Hodder Headline. Ben is now well established as a novelist and writer of TV dramas. The competition ran for four years and judges included award-winning authors Anne Cassidy, Iain Sinclair, Ardashir Vakil and Elizabeth Waite.

Congratulations to James Mitchell, the winner in 2019,

and all the longlisted writers.

We hope the 2019 Brick Lane Bookshop Short Story Prize will be the first of many to come.

Denise Jones
Brick Lane Bookshop

Introduction

Kate Ellis

Back in 2015, I met Ali Smith at a book launch and apropos of I can't remember what, told her about a taxidermied Jack Russell I saw at Spitalfields Market and as I was thinking how odd it was to stuff a pet, it snorted and made me jump. Later, I sourced Ali's email address and asked if she would judge the short story competition I was running. She replied, albeit with a gracious no, and said she remembered my 'unstuffy dog story', which made me happier than a yes.

All fairly irrelevant, and if this introduction were a short story, I would – as many editors advise – delete the first paragraph. I'm going to leave it because it gives background and goes some way to showing how long I have been mulling over creating a short story prize. That was going to be the East London Short Story Prize, for which I designed a logo but failed to apply for Arts Council funding. Four years on, Brick Lane Bookshop has funded the prize, so it now exists. Which is great.

I've entered many short story competitions, so I know what attracts writers to submit: a cash prize, excellent judges and the possibility of publication. I'm yet to win a competition, perhaps because my editing abilities are shoddy (see above), but I've been lucky enough to be longlisted, shortlisted and published. Each time I get an email letting me know my story has progressed past the slush pile, it gives me hope that I'm not completely mad to type thoughts into my laptop first thing in the morning. It validates me and allows me to begin to believe I am a writer. That identity is a difficult thing to establish when you work alone in made-up worlds with people, creatures or events that only exist in your own mind.

Being longlisted means at least one stranger has read your work and rates it. It allows hope to momentarily creep past the doubt. Ergo: prizes are important. They help writers to continue and to write more and better. Their winnings might buy them a few pints, or a week on a retreat, or a laptop with a functional letter 'E'. Their work might be read by more strangers, be sent to agents, or find its way to bookshelves. There could be an event where writers meet some people who've read their work and talk about their characters as if they're real and this could make the writer feel warm and fuzzy inside. Then there's rejection. This is less obviously positive but still useful. It hurts and makes you angry, then sad, then despondent, then determined. These emotions, if you're lucky, can be redirected into motivation to re-edit or resend work to a new prize where it will encounter a different set of first readers who are having different days to the previous bunch. All 463 entries were read at least twice by a team of eleven. The diversity of stories and opinions about those stories was incredible. The entries created a strange portrait of a nation. Repeated themes included homelessness, violence, dystopia, anxiety, online dating, misogyny and escape, to name a few.

To begin writing a short story, you have to be brave enough to make yourself vulnerable, to let your thoughts run free. You also have to show what your characters are like while economically convincing your reader this is a story they should care about. You must also have the audacity to ask questions you don't know the answer to. You not only aim to convince your reader, in a few thousand words, your story is worthy of their attention and precious time, but hope that, by the end, they're altered, tipped off kilter, shown a different perspective or brought to laughter or tears. It's a difficult task.

The stories in this anthology build worlds and establish voices within a few lines. These writers are not afraid of appearing peculiar or harsh. They mine their own experience and stretch their imaginations, repurpose acute observations for fiction. They leave us with questions about both their story's world and our real one.

Short stories don't arrive fully formed and polished. They take a long time and a lot of head space. All the more reason to reward those that work. In this anthology you'll read about finite tears, kidnapping, race riots, obsessive running, chicken guts, sand, grief, friendship, jellyfish, magpies, caregiving and council housing amongst other things.

At Brick Lane Bookshop, we're celebrating the short

story because that means celebrating ideas, creativity, curiosity and imagination. It means reading voices we've never heard before and stories from places we've never been. In 2019, more than ever, this is vital.

Kate Ellis
Bookseller and project manager of the Brick Lane
Bookshop Short Story Prize

**Brick Lane Bookshop
Short Story Prize**
Longlist 2019

A Body Is an Empty Vessel

James Mitchell

Youth Pastor John will spend most of the service saying that Ruth has found her better place, which is exactly what we want to hear. People only ever care about what's in it for them. They're happy to let the low-calorie Body of Christ save their souls, but they'd rather not think about how it's made. Nobody wants to imagine some factory pumping out God-body wafers, nobody wants to think about how the Cry Booth works, and they definitely don't want to think about what'll happen to Ruth's body when her coffin goes into the Somerton soil.

I shut my eyes and try to really picture the worms between her long fingers, the ground's oil matting that dark hair, and wait for tears to flow. Regret doesn't come in any other language for Mom and Dad: when I showed them the one purple fingernail I painted this morning, to remember, Dad asked why I'd adorned my own body. Today, Ruth has shiny pink-varnished nails because a dead body is public property, dressed the way and lying the way the family wants it to. Everyone's got what they wanted from her big day, except her.

My cheeks are flushing.

Am I crying?

No. It's not going to come from a purple nail.

And now Youth Pastor John begins: 'Ruth Simmons, "Ruthie" to her friends, was a passionate girl who touched the lives of all who knew her.' He clasps his knuckles. 'In just three months since joining our Somerton flock, she'd collected a circle of girls who cared for her, and were slowly bringing her closer to God when disaster came.' He says these things and more things like them, and everyone gathered in the Mission's hall hangs on all of it, even though every word is straight from the book of Youth Funeral Clichés. A cliché is something you say or do over and over again until it's lost its power. That's one of the things she taught me.

He says: 'We're now going to hear a few words from someone who knew her best.' I take a deep breath and stand, and the congregation turns to face me at the back.

No, of course I don't. Up jumps Tall Carly. Youth Pastor John smiles and gives her his place at the lectern. There are a few coughs, one from Mom who's actually trying not to cry, but gets to do it anyway. The Cry Booth people hate Mom's kind, freeloaders born with more tears than the rest of us. Dad squeezes my hand in a supportive way. I throw him off. Tall Carly takes a pink notecard out of a pocket in her shorts.

'Ruthie was like, really special to us?'

To Tall Carly's right, the cluster of cheerleaders, drawn up like bridesmaids at Youth Pastor John's request, nod in sync. Of the five, two are already weeping. They're also the pair who rejected Ruth when she walked into the Mission on her first day in Somerton. But they've got the tears, and I haven't. Not any more.

~

The first thing a newcomer needs to know about the Kids Enjoy, Kids Endure Faith Mission is that the smell of turpentine is not going to go away, but you can get used to it. The second thing is that we find it hard to deal with new people. So when Ruth Simmons walked up to our circle of folding chairs, trying to wave the smell from her nose with the brim of a black hat, only Youth Pastor John followed his holy mission and said, 'Welcome! Why don't you have a seat next to Connie?'

'Constance,' I greeted her, because 'Connie' is something you share when it suits you. That Sunday we were talking about Temperance. I say 'we' but it's Youth Pastor John who does the talking, rolling his shirt cuffs up and down his arms depending on how much he's trying to connect with us. When he reached 'Temperance is what makes it cool to say "No Thanks"', the hints of upper arm made Tall Carly and Simone practically melt into their fold-up chairs, so unavailable was he. That's when Ruth made the first sound anyone had heard from her. A single 'Hah!' then a little girly-piggy snort like the laughter had been building from the moment she saw all of us, and the flash of chaste bicep had pushed her over the edge. The circle glared at us, and I first felt something unpeel.

Salvation comes at twelve on Sundays, so there's normally just enough time for me to bike over to Mary's Kitchen ('Where Your Table's Always Saved!') to meet Mom and Dad, but they were out of town at another conference so I walked Ruth out, hoping to instruct her how to better Enjoy and Endure the meetings.

'When it comes to sermon time, find yourself something

3

to stare at that isn't too boring, but won't get you in trouble if you're caught.'

'No guys, then?'

'Joshua and Isaac?' I'd never thought of them as anything more than tall versions of the boys I'd grown up with; chinos and good manners. 'They're not . . .'

Ruth adjusted her hat, but I couldn't see much difference. 'Then what do you look at?'

'I make shapes with the pattern in the ceiling.'

'Let them think you're talking to the Almighty?'

'Who says I'm not?'

'God in a triangle.' She pouted like a French philosopher. 'Tray jolee.'

I felt responsible for her view of the town, so I showed her the drive-in movie, the megachurch, and the creek where we all used to hang out before we got old and it got dry. She didn't look impressed, so we weaved through the shiny L of the Somerton Mall. As we walked down the long side she explained how they'd had to move to the area from New York, following her dad's job, and she was going to the Mission to help her college application, gather those faith scholarships to plough into a critical philosophy major.

I bought her a cinnamon pretzel, and a Mountain Dew Code Red for myself. Additives be d***ed, it pulls me back to life in the hot part of the day. She said her mom thought soft drinks were the devil, then she blushed. I offered her a swig. She tasted a drop, then chugged half the bottle. Ruby ooze slid along the seam of her bottom lip. That's when I first noticed the pout she showed at a new experience, the sense that something hadn't quite lived up to her fantasies; a dare to find something that could.

'Do you really buh-lieve, though, Constance?'

'Of course,' I said. 'Don't you?'

'Well,' she said, and pulled the knot straight out of the middle of her pretzel, 'whoever's out there, I'd love to meet him. Ask him about wars and famine.' She ate the knot in one bite and tossed the leftover ring away. 'I just don't think he's made from yeast or whatever.'

There was a pile-up in my brain between the Witnessing dialogue for moments like this, and the things you say to a new friend, so I just finished the Code Red. It was four, nearly time for me to clock on. Chinese kids' English homework doesn't ghostwrite itself. But Ruth was already pulling me down the stubby part of the L. Her deep-purple nails dragged me to a booth I hadn't seen before, next to the Forever 21. She pouted up her nose at the pink lettering.

'"Cry Booth"?'

And now everyone's heard of them, sure, but just this one time I like to think Somerton got there first. It was like those Otaku Photo Booths that draw you with big eyes or a halo or a cartoon flying cat on your shoulder. A sticker read:

$5 = 5 MINS :'(

– which felt like a lot for some fortune-teller thing. I only get $10 per essay. The inside was high and narrow, squashing us together on a stool so our thighs touched to the knee. Ruth pulled the curtain across and we first smelt that Cry Booth smell: lavender, cedar balls and a splash of TCP. The walls inside that first booth we tried were radioactive bubblegum pink. They know their audience – it's a mall, right? I'm

5

sure the ones that popped up in hospital waiting rooms were medical green, and the ones in office canteens were a cubicle beige, but this one was a girl's pencil case, and when Ruth drummed her nails on it they stood out like a drop of blood in olive oil.

There was a screen, but it didn't show us, like a normal booth would. It only showed moving colours and shapes like one of those '90s screensavers on the Mission computer. When it reached the end of whatever demo it was running, it flickered black before starting again. In that moment our faces were shown to us in the mirror, but I wasn't looking at my own reflection. I was looking at Ruth's.

She pushed $5 into the slot, sharply creased in the middle from its time in a chic black-patent wallet in her butt pocket. The slot spat it out, and right there we should have got up and walked away. But I didn't want to get up, didn't want her to get up. So I smoothed it out on my leggings, and tried it once again.

Once it got popular, people would say all sorts of dumb things about how the Cry Booth worked – it used your DNA, or the NSA, or hypnosis or pheromones – but not in the first month. As the booths popped up across the town, the gossip was all about the strange thing it did to you. You'd have been laughing about, say, some goofy homebrew proverb from Youth Pastor John, or the way Isaac's voice wobbled when he did Purity Role-Play with Tall Carly, or just checking your phone – and then suddenly you wouldn't care about any of that stuff.

Your chest would go heavy, your eyes would blink as your thoughts of Chinese homework or melting ice caps or college scholarships flew away and you'd start to breathe faster, and that huge dam that had been filling up quietly inside you would break, and natural as anything, you just cried. Real sobbing, authentic tears. You'd cry about your no thigh gap, and your no boyfriend, and the way Tall Carly and friends ignored you. 'Ruth, what's happening?' you'd say. One time, you'd find yourself saying 'Ruthie'.

As the booth shifted up, sorrow lost perspective, and you'd be crying for your mom and dad, then for the world, then yourself, then Ruthie's nail polish and then black and then nothing, nothing at all.

And out of the darkness, the Cry Booth would make a sound like a bicycle bell and you'd just be two girls in a little pink box, holding each other.

That's what five dollars bought you, every time.

~

'Let's bow our heads together in reflection,' says Youth Pastor John. Mom huffs next to me. Later she'll say, 'Constance, I am all for reaching out to the young and unsaved like poor Ruth, but we're going to have to call it what it is, and that is capital-P Prayer, plain and simple.' But today I'm not Praying or even Reflecting. I just watch the body. It's right there, Ruthie not moving. Ruthie not holding my hand, Ruthie not painting my nails and explaining about *cherchez la femme*, and how I was *la femme*. Now Youth Pastor John says: 'Every tear is a messenger dove flown from the soul, when it's truly earned.' He's trying to catch my eye but I won't let him. Today, the pattern in the ceiling looks like doves fighting or having sex or calling it all off.

7

He raises his voice and his hands, asking us to give Ruth our thanks for a reminder of the sweetness of genuine grief. Her parents grip folds in each other's clothing. People make little sobs from the front of the hall, and I wait for the wave to strike me. My breath catches in my chest. Inside my pocket, my purple nail digs into my palm. The pain makes me wince but still, dry eyes. Even Youth Pastor John is tearing up; so much for Temperance. This has got to be his biggest moment. A parking-lot-vigil, nation-in-mourning death of 'an *innocent fifteen-year-old*', he says. 'Killed by the Cry Booth, by the emotional indulgence of a dark TV tarot: The Apprentice, The Swan, The Bachelor. A Godless society that cannot understand pain,' he says. 'Pain is quiet, pain is patient, pain endures all the –'

Even the ceiling doves seem to be weeping now and John keeps twisting the knife, John on Pain, John the Dickless. He says, 'Does anyone wish to express their private grief with the hall?' His wet gaze flits over me. The parents at the funeral lap it all up, and the anger bubbles in me but still chokes at the gate. No tears.

~

On the hot Friday night after Homecoming, lonely and drunk on a bottle of peach schnapps she'd stolen from her mom, Ruthie and I went on one of our two-hour Cry Booth binges. A campus booth, rigged up behind the sports hall and painted in team colours. We swigged and sobbed and pumped money in until our chests ached. Twenty dollars, thirty-five. Money I was saving for the collection plate.

At fifty dollars, it stopped working. Ruthie pushed all

her bills into the slot, then all mine. The Cry Booth whirred, TCP'd, bicycle-belled, but neither of us was so much as sniffling.

'Come ON!' Ruthie yelled, and smashed the flat of her hand against the screen picture of Crying Taylor Swift.

A face peeped round the curtain. 'Hey, be careful?'

It was Tall Carly, which meant the rest of the squad would be behind her, queuing in order of seniority, second-string offensive linesmen smoking behind them. Looking for release after their big performance, equal parts pompoms and parables.

'Oh, it's you.'

I took a breath to apologise or explain or possibly try to put my face through the glass. Ruthie peered up at the floating head.

'Carly,' she drawled. 'Finished sucking Reverend John's dick already?'

'He's *Youth Pas-tor*, Marie Antoinette. And he's not, I mean I wouldn't . . .'

She turned her broad blond face to me. 'What are you still doing with this specimen, Connie? You used to be healthy.'

I was about to laugh it off in that way that lets both people pretend they've won the argument, when Ruthie's fist shot out, clenched the shoulder strap of Tall Carly's cheer vest, and pulled her into the booth. The smell of peach encircled us all.

'First, fuck the fuck off. Second,' and I felt her other hand on my shoulder, 'it's Constance.'

And she shoved Tall Carly and her absurdly high centre of gravity right out of the booth. It suddenly felt smaller than it ever had, Ruthie's New York hips jabbing pleasantly into mine. I turned to her, laughing drunk, and then suddenly not laughing, and feeling more sober than ever because she was just so –

Tall Carly pulled back the curtain to reveal the whole cheer line, and smiled at Ruthie.

'You don't belong here,' she said.

Then she left, they all left, and pretty soon the Cry Booth went *zhing*, and it was over.

Next day, the local news was calling it 'Tearless'. We heard it in snatches of conversation as we spent my whole week's wage (three term papers and an admissions letter) in different booths around town, even the new one outside the homeless shelter that did fifteen seconds for a quarter.

A pair of off-duty Montvale cops had looked in on a booth in the back of a failing strip club, the night before. They opened the red curtain to find a businessman lying on the floor, body bent around the stool, swimming in damp five-dollar bills and smelling of whisky. When they woke him, he said his wife had left him for a motivational speaker who'd won a bronze in Atlanta '96, so he'd gone into the booth with a bottle of rye and a money clip of fives. After sixteen hours, his tear ducts had dried up. Then a sociologist called in to KLAX95.2 claiming that the average person cries for three weeks of their life, if you push it all together. Finally, an anonymous blogger who'd supposedly worked on the Cry Booths and then been fired claimed that pushing all the crying together was exactly what the booth did. It took all the tears someone had left to shed in their life and brought them forward like a loan, till they were spent. After that and for evermore, your waterworks were as gone as the Californian water table.

We read that part on our phones, sat on a wall watching people pass through the drive-thru Cry Lane by the golf course. I felt Ruthie's hand shake in mine. Her cheeks shone, but it was only sweat.

Being Tearless is to live in a world with a little less oxygen than everyone else. When you're sad, you feel trapped on the edge of sneezing, clenched toes, mouth open, eyes open. If you're not sad you can forget about it. Like tinnitus. It's only in the quiet that you remember a little part of your senses is cut away for ever. How you're going to graduate with an Easter Island face, to read *The Fault in Our Stars* in silence, to bury your parents with the visible grief of a headstone.

An SUV rolled past us, the driver shaking her head with personal revelation, and I saw Ruthie dig at the dust with her heels until one broke. I asked her how she felt, because I could no longer tell. But nor could she.

~

Maybe it's the smell, but the congregation's too keen to jump up and hurry over to the wake. Some carry their floral tributes with them, too important to be left with a body. Youth Pastor John rushes to the door to thank people on the way out, his Mission business cards in hand like communion. Your parents follow, holding hands. Mom and Dad give me a look, but I wave at them to go on ahead.

A pause. They do.

Now it's just me and you, Ruthie. This time I know you're gone. Maybe you always were: you said we'd never booth alone, but when your parents called looking for you, it didn't take the divine to know where you'd be. You'd borrowed

11

enough money off me, and I'd been happy to lend it knowing I'd ride in your pocket for the rest of the day. When I walked into that very first booth we tried and saw you on the floor, cuddling a bottle of Vicodin like a teddy bear, I thought you'd fallen asleep pumping money in like the lonely businessman.

The way they've made you up in the casket, you could just be dozing, put to sleep by Youth Pastor John's eulogy. Your mom's rouged your cheeks, the way you did yourself – and some angel has quietly given you a hint of the smoky-eye thing you once gave me.

The door clicks open behind us, and Tall Carly ducks her head round. She looks at the floor, then at me.

'I'm sorry, Connie,' she says, then she's gone.

The casket is huge. Your mom chose something expensive, and it makes you look tiny in the way you always wanted. *La femme*. With your hands clasped over your heart as if to say, '*Moi?*'

I reach down and take your hand. Not feeling for a pulse any more but just holding you, letting you feel my warmth. I open your hands and run my one purple fingernail along the crease you told me was called your lifeline. The line seems to run down your wrist and right to your heart, out of my reach from here. I can see your parents through a window, shaking hands and pointing the way to the wake. They'll be back any minute to close the heavy lid over you, for ever.

Forgive me. That's what I'll say when I'm found; it's all I can say. But this is what you'd do, Ruthie, if you had no other way to show how you feel. I slip my flats off, and climb into the casket.

It's tighter on the inside; your hip still presses into me. With my fingers laced between yours, your hand feels a little

12

tense, like any moment it'll grip mine and you'll climb out and drag me to another booth in a new town. But this one's good enough for us. From the inside, looking up, the ceiling's pattern is like stars in daylight, or the closing pores in your face. Someone's left a blind open. The sun's slipping beneath it, so your skin is warm as we lie there cheek against cheek.

That circle of chairs. They couldn't look away. You walked in here a woman.

My breath catches in the familiar way. I am on the edge again.

But then – It can't be. It's got to be a speck of sawdust, or your long eyelashes on mine, but now I'm blinking, and I'm shaking, and –

There. My cheek, it's wet.

I pull away to show you.

And I see it.

Your smoky make-up has trickled down, a black vein.

It's you.

Life with Animals

Rosanna Hildyard

February: lambing time. Blood in the fields. What should be inside is turned out: placentas float in pools of urine where the bladder has collapsed after birth. Shaggy ewes stand stock still like frosted garden furniture. They are streaked with mud and blood and faded turquoise, cherry or purple according to which ram, wearing a strap-on bag of coloured chalk, tupped them. Tupped: sounds innocent enough. But we are the girls who have grown up round here. Here, in this garrison town sprawled across a moor. We know what's underneath that word.

February: twilight at three thirty. A girl is running down the lines between fields. If you paused at the top of the hill road, on your way off somewhere, you'd just be able to make her out: the mechanical rhythm of her Lycraed legs, the bobbing of her head above her slight shoulders. The husk of her ribcage heaves visibly in and out, iPod jutting from the pocket at her tail. Even from this distance, you'd be able to see the girl is all bone. She's what we would call at school *too skinny*, sucking in our cheeks. She must weigh about six stone, by this point, we'd say, if we had to guess. She is alone.

We left sixth form in June. Most of us are still here. Living in this spiral of housing estates and barracks; sleeping in childhood bedrooms decorated with *Playboy* wallpaper, sharing a bunk bed with a younger sister. Most of the boys joined the army; we work in Tesco, or the gym, or the pub, or the Chinese. One or two of us went off to university but for the most part we wait, put off the decision, for one more year at least. Our legs are still covered with scratches from misdirected razor blades and the hedges at the back of the park. We only recently started padding ourselves against leaks and lumps; reading magazines that address us as a group: *you*. Our breasts are in full flower, but only just. We aren't quite ready to live our lives apart from each other.

We know she jogs the same loop every day, in the afternoon before dark. We're reminded of her Lycra and caving hipbones as we sit in each other's warm kitchens, happening to glance out of the window at the cold sky. She'll be easier to track than a fox or a badger, one of us mutters, while nursing a mug of tea. We swap stories about the sort of men who hang around in those woods where she runs: men with only a dog for company and only Sky Sports to come back to. A man who would easily be able to disappear if he wanted. It's not what she should be doing, we all agree. When she started, last summer, back when she was still one of us, we cornered her in the Wetherspoons toilets and hissed at her about it – *It's not safe!* – but she carried on, anyway, as if she didn't care.

The neon-pink stripes of her leggings make a sharp flash against the fields and clouds, if you happen to be walking home around the edge of the estate. Even the sheep look up and shuffle where they are crowded in their pens. White and folded together, they look like the arms and legs jumbled in the creases of those magazines. The girl running might steal a glance at them, and we'd be fairly sure we'd know what she's thinking: Do they mind which ram tupped them? Do they even know?

The sheep look back calmly, bleeding under the trees.

Boys at school and around the garrison started watching us about the same time as our bodies started lurching and gathering. That was why we first started examining ourselves as well, as we recall. Stomach pressed in, for a reflection. Testing the effect of Barry M glitter nail varnish, on fingers flung out to drum on a desk. The boys – Matthew, Lewis, Jack – all with their eyes keen on a piece of our backs, hands, arms.

She slogs uphill, past the Coast to Coast signpost, its yellow arrow exclaiming at the sheep. Pushes forward. She must have been running and halting and gasping and starting again for nearly an hour. She's on the last stretch, now. We sneer at the hikers who sometimes stop at the estate pub. They leer over the sticky bar and congratulate those of us behind it on the beautiful countryside. But they're thinking of fields of waving corn, not sheep trailing ribbons of afterbirth through their own shit. We smile and bring them their gin and tonic, and they don't look up to thank us, too busy swaggering on to each other. Views this, rewilding that. They don't see that men like our dads are flooding the land with acids and drenches and injections, desperately tamping it down for the supermarkets' perfectionist judgement.

As we started bleeding, certain of us began to be led outside at the house parties, then more. First Rhiannon, then Katie. Even when we liked it, when we were sitting on Sam, or Jamie, or Matthew, we knew to watch ourselves.

She fails on the hill, rasps to a halt. Has to stand by the roadside gulping in more clean air till her body has the energy to start up again. In those leggings, you can see her legs are as thin as a bike's inner tubes. We know even her bones are light. We were there, sitting in Lydia's bedroom – fug of cheese and onion, lipgloss and cigarettes – when she got the osteopenia result from the NHS, by text. Katie grabbed the phone from her dry twiggy hands and passed it around, gasping, and we egged her on to eat a packet of crisps. She'd mostly stopped seeing us by then, of course. She'd only come round because at Lydia's we could smoke. After the crisps, she stopped entirely.

She runs twice a day and only eats fruit, even though she's obviously hungry. She said to us, at the beginning, that she just wanted to be able to make her body how she wanted it; get on top of it. *On top*, we sniggered: like the boys said Rhiannon always tried. We sometimes see her mother about, in Tesco or bent over her bags in the street. We call: 'Hello, Mrs C!' And, if she hears us (which she often doesn't, wrapped up in her own thoughts as she often is), she'll look up and give a wobbly smile through lips pressed ice-cream white. 'Oh, hello, girls.'

The light is leaving the fields now, and the wind must be cutting into her with a new chill – look, she's shiny with sweat. The moon low in the sink of the sky. She stands, shakes her head and jerks it, spitting towards the hedge, and then freezes, her attention caught by something at its root. Her whole body is tense, focused towards – what is it? We can't see. After a moment, she takes a cautious step closer to the ditch. And another – then halts, face twisting like she's felt some bad smell wedging into her nostrils, and we realise: just a dead or dying animal, probably a myxie rabbit, lying in tyre grooves at the side of the road. There are plenty. We can imagine it: bloody tidemarks of foam on its sides, pawing at a puddle. It has no idea what is happening to it. It doesn't care. An invisible prison has descended onto it, white pain slashing away all sound.

She stands there for a minute, watching. Wet fur and spasms. One of the boys might have felt sorry for it, broken a stick off the hedgerow and thumped the head till it caved in – the skull can't be thicker than a DVD box. She doesn't. She watches, arms folded, as it lies dying, not understanding what has happened to make its legs jerk and lungs drown from inside.

She turns away, walks a few paces and breaks back into a jog.

The boys don't much like it if you murmur and make noises. You pay attention; don't let yourself go. Jack had said to her to stop wriggling about, that night at Kieran's he'd had his hand hard on the crotch of her jeans. We whispered about it, afterwards, and she said she'd felt something hot, like a buzz, and hadn't been able to stop herself from jumping. Wow, all right, we'd said. You couldn't control yourself?

On, and her breath makes a harsh sound on the silent road. Her ears are red and there's snot on her nose. But she's always cold, these days. When we see her, we look coldly: her wrists stick out of her bomber jacket at weird angles and there is thick hair on them. Gross, we think. We feel sorry for her, for looking like that.

We became aware, at these parties, reading the magazines, that we had to look and feel right. We dreaded that his hands

19

might suddenly find damp in our armpits or thighs, or that his poking fingers might press something to shock us into a moan – deeper than we'd have thought our voices could be – and the next day at school they'd all be mimicking the sounds that had come out. We'd hear the boys calling from across the college car park, like whistling a bird's call. We walked quicker, narrowed our eyes at each other as we worked out which of us it was.

When she started, we told her repeatedly: Boys don't like girls too skinny, it doesn't look good! But it seemed as if she just didn't care. One thing she did keep talking about was cleaning it. We talked more about make-up; wore our pancake faces all alike. Detoxifying, blemish-free, radiant, good, beautiful – is what it said on our creams and scrubs, and what we repeated. At first, even her mother said, 'You're so *good*,' admiringly, when we were round hers for dinner, when we turned to her and she led us in a chorus of: 'No dessert, thanks, we're on a diet.' People around here still look at her, but in a different way, now.

She passes under the first orange streetlight of the estate and past the slutty Metcalfes' house, who we stopped talking to when Leanne Metcalfe got with Liam, who was going with Hayley. Past the house where Mrs Jimmy died and the one where the pervy old man lives – he must be, with *Star Wars* Lego filling every window, always the same, ever since we were born. Not many of us have left: Katherine, Jack, Sophie came back from uni at Christmas different, with new clothes and a new edge to their voice. The boys who'd joined the army came back, too, from their training camp. Some louder, some quieter, but all with shaven heads.

She stops at the corner shop, as she often does. The bell

doesn't clink as she slips through the door, barely pushing it open more than a foot. One boy is leaning on the counter, the other is behind it. Both turn to gawp, then turn back to meet each other's eyes. The sweat is trickling down her neck; they can see. She stares, then spins abruptly around and walks towards the milk. A soft snigger reaches her ears.

— 'ing every day.
— She think it looks good?
— Running all the time.
— Dunno, but you know Lewis . . .

We used to make a big fuss about how none of us liked cow's milk much. *Think what it comes from!* we used to shriek in disgust. At a party once, Lewis made a joke about the first man to discover cow's milk: What was he doing? If we ever catch her in this dusty old shop, murmuring quickly under her breath (*Soya is 44 kcal per 100 ml. Skim: 33 kcal per 100 ml.*), she'll blush and hurry away.

We all knew Lewis. He's popular for being on the football team, and, what's more, he's nice. A rare one. We'd gossip about him: Why didn't he go with a girl, regular? She told us about Lewis on his bed, after, while she was doing her bra up: gentle eyes, his blond hair sticking up because she'd gripped it. Neither of them had done it much before, we guessed. They didn't speak much after that time – only the third – because they were both awkward. She was weird: she only said she'd messed up. And he was always a quiet one. Then classes stopped for summer revision, and she'd stopped talking about anything except make-up and cleanliness really, by then.

Louise and Sophie were joking with him, over Christmas, asked if he'd seen her. Not since the last time, he said, and looked kind and embarrassed. She'd bled, he said, and didn't realise. What? she'd said, when he told her. He'd thought he should tell her only so she could take care of it.

Watch out for yourself, he'd said. You take care, now. He'd let her out the front door himself, in full view of the street, and asked to walk her home, but she wouldn't let him. He said to Louise and Sophie that he wouldn't have told anyone, but now he thinks she must've been really upset, for some reason.

She walks to the freezer and slides it open with a loud groan; the ice puffs out. She closes her eyes and holds her hot, pulsing face above. The boys are whispering:

— Bled.

Or was it:

— Bed.
— Mmm – fuck –

Another soft snigger. The door clinks shut after her. Her cheeks red, hot.

If we weren't drinking, we were eating. When we laughed, you could see our mouths full of white crisp mulch and red gum stuck in our teeth. Fizzy sweets were always squashed at the bottom of our rucksacks, to be passed under desks during lessons. While watching TV (in the dim caves of our sitting rooms, at the height of summer), we'd be mindlessly crunching packets of chocolate digestives and half-heartedly saying, 'Get that away from me!' throwing them across the room. Oven pizzas always came out at a certain point in the house parties: Dr. Oetker's Ristorante, with those flat slices of cheese and tomato sauce that had never seen a tomato plant. Chips laden with gravy burning fingers at the bus stop after a night out. In Hayley's kitchen, the last time she'd come round for tea, she'd only pushed the sweet potato curry around the plate and we heard her stomach rumble. Hayley asked if she wanted some bread and tricked her by bringing out ice cream; we knew what she was up to. She had to sit on her hands when Hayley held up the ice-cream scoop. She looked at us pleadingly, but we were unmoved. It was for her own good. We knew that she had to be normal. We liked the same things, we did the same things; what was unsafe was being outside – Leanne, Rhiannon. We were trying to help.

She continues on, up to the roundabout and the main road. Thump, thump, the balls and the heels of her feet. The same small surprise of recognising the same H-shaped crack in the tarmac she sees every day and forgets a second afterwards.

We used to look at each other and then at ourselves and watch what we did with our bodies, with the boys. At Jack's or Cameron's house parties, at sleepovers. In the daytime, we sauntered along the lino corridors with breathy greetings for the teachers. We'd put a comforting arm around her and tell her to treat herself. We didn't know what our bodies wanted, really, on those nights when we copied each other. Mostly, we felt like rubber being handled and lifted around. The occasional electric jolt of pleasure from someone running their fingers lightly down your back.

Once, a boy stroking your hair.

But it changed quickly, who laid claim to which boy – it

was not clear-cut and we didn't want to upset anyone in the group. Sisters before misters, we told each other. Boys we went to primary school with – Nick, Tom – stroking us in someone's garden, in the dark. Each on a different night; it didn't matter who.

We watch her running on, in the dark, past our houses. We look out of the curtains and blink. She must be starving, exhausted. She somehow manages to force her legs to keep moving, on and on. What she gets out of it, we can't understand, and we shake our heads as we look at her, deflated and trembling, heading up towards the main road. Perhaps she's paying for yesterday, when she gave in. We'd spotted her, walking across from the library (where she often is: it's away from her parents and the fridge, isn't it) to the Co-op, where she purchased a reduced-price tuna mayonnaise sandwich for 80p. Bit into it before she'd even made it through the doors, the cashier told us.

What kind of hunger she must have felt, to drool like that over a few bits of sugary supermarket bread and some piss-smelling brown paste. She managed to stop herself there. She must've tried to think hard of the bleeding, tin eyes turned into fleshy mush, which then became part of her own body – *dirty, mucky*, as she would say. But, still, her hands couldn't let the food go. We could see the thin snail-trail of spittle ooze from the corner of her mouth, and watched as she walked briskly back into the library, headed to the grubby toilets. Must have taken a few short, sharp breaths of the stench in there, eyes watering over a toilet full up with someone's brownish, flecked urine, and then felt sick, and been able to throw the sandwich away. Gain some sort of control over herself again.

She is stumbling on down the dual carriageway now, by

the exit of the estate. Polluted air and tyre smell on her left; on her right, lit windows, people moving about their kitchens. She runs right past Lydia's house, and has to stop. She must have to; we know she doesn't want to stop here. All out of gas. Has to lean on Lydia's fence, which Lydia's dad painted the colour of ox-blood, and stare at the ground.

Headlights from the road rough over her and flee away. One way leads to the motorway. The other, back to the garrison, its supermarkets and spiralling estates, the multiplex and leisure centre, the barracks; and then, further, moorlands, bike paths, and stout walking couples, heather and grouse; and, further, we don't know.

People are the same everywhere; we know.

She looks into the road and into the headlights, her tired shoulders moving up and down with her breath, then can't meet their bright gaze any longer; can no longer bear whatever she's imagining. Drops her head and turns to walk slowly away, towards home.

At Hayley's, she might hear the echo of a whisper: *Look, there she goes*. Last time she saw a group of us, we were waiting for the bus before a night out. Sitting on that wall right there, chewing gum and passing a bottle of white rum between us. She walked straight past, keeping her eyes fixed ahead. You could see the curve of her spine under her jumper, thick as a lizard's tail. Wrists that could stop a grown man in his tracks.

Our legs lay propped and bare over the pavement, biscuit with fake tan, suncream smeared over our moles. One of us had whispered – Louise, probably, or Katie – and she'd twisted her heavy head back towards us, only to be met with our breezy smiles. Our smooth, shaven legs stretched out, blocking her way back.

There are two ways to go: a slut or boring. We can't help thinking, now, that we'd always known, deep down, that one of them would happen to her. You can always tell who is slightly on the edge of the group, the last to be chosen for a pair. Frigid bitch, cocktease: that was the worst thing to be. We all know that you have to be fun; you had to do what the boys wanted – just, not too much.

At her back gate now. Tufts of grass growing around it. She stops and we watch as she flicks a woodlouse off the handle, a miniscule ping. She places her shoulder against the door and heaves, creaks it open and pulls herself through.

There is a bowl of giblets outside the back door; her dad must've been on the shoot. It's a hobby for older men – our dads who are ex-army or work on the land. Only a tenner subscription, and they go to the pub after. This year, there were too many pheasants. The shooters tramping from house to house on the estate, ringing the doorbell and offering the soft, bleeding bodies like some Hallowe'en in reverse. They bagged so many that they ended up chucking the birds in the tip, or burying them on the farms. We cried off, when our mothers offered stewed pheasant for tea – 'Yuk, we're vegetarian' – and our mothers told us some people would be grateful for free meat.

These shot pheasants are old and tough. They have dandruff and their guts are bursting with black, stringy shit. She and her mum have to pluck the ones her dad brings home. When she's gutting them, she puts the organs aside as feed for the magpies in her dad's traps – a magpie trap holds a live magpie as bait to catch others. Magpies are bad for farmers; chicken-killers, cannibal egg-drinkers. That's the sort of thing ramblers saluting pretty, glittery birds don't know.

She bends to look over the bowl on the step. Damp pheasant feathers and traces of dried-up cat food, which is what the magpies eat when there's no pheasant, cling to the slippery mauve giblets. Rimmed with a touch of primrose fat. She touches the bowl with her foot, furtively, and it wobbles. Fat. Fragile. Pregnant stomachs, pretty brown driblets like slug antennae and soft-boiled eggs breaking up into kidney soup.

That's what's inside her, inside all of us, right now: those fructifying globes and balls puttering along on their own processes without us being able to do anything about it. We all look the same on the inside, all of us filled with identical organs. Fragile. There is no way to tell, from looking at silk smoothness and freckles, what is going on underneath your own skin.

Each of us girls has once woken in her own childhood bed, in a pool of her own blood.

Maybe it was better to be a frigid bitch, weirdo, cocktease, than to end up like Rhiannon who took turns with all of the boys, everywhere; in the toilets and the field, head after head. Rhiannon shouts and swears at us whenever she sees us around. The skin on her face is beginning to look like a tongue.

If one of us, or one of the boys – Luke, Lewis, Cameron – told us to quieten down and get a hold of ourselves, how would we know how?

She sticks a hand inside her sweaty leggings and fishes out the key. Opens the back door, shutting it carefully behind her with a soft click. We see her shadow moving away through the frosted glass. We wait. We look up at her bedroom window. We can only see closed curtains. But we know she'll be able to see the moon through the skylight from where she lies spreadeagled on her bed. A sob is a coiled spring in her chest.

We'll watch out for her. We are worried about her. *She needs to realise*, we say, scandalised, to each other. But we're sure she will realise, soon enough. She'll realise that she doesn't like being looked at in the way we look at her now, in nose-wrinkling, sympathetic disgust. In the way the boys look at her, with a swallowed, nervous giggle, their eyes deliberately sliding away from hers. She'll realise that you are looked at, whatever happens.

And anyway, she'll become too hungry. She will have to learn, slowly, how to eat again. The flesh will thicken and ripen across her bones, she will apply fake tan: apricot. Her parents will breathe a sigh of relief and start nagging her again. And we will glide to her, one day, down the aisle of the bus, and drop down on the seats beside and in front of her, and offer gum or a fag, and she will be back safe; one of the group again.

She will wiggle herself into a bodycon skirt, the same as the rest. She will sneak out to meet us in a dark garden. She will watch the sparks and flames fly into the stars and drink until it all becomes a haze and she stops thinking, and the boy whose lap she is sitting in will pinch her bum and tell her to keep still, and she will try to hold her stomach in and smile; watching, as the faces of the boys and girls around her blur and mould into one.

Hot Butter on Repeat

Judith Wilson

A sharp Liverpool wind. Bins tumble.

Bernadette thinks this. Doesn't look up.

'Tea's ready.'

It's not, but she shouts to Brian anyway, words over her shoulder like a dishcloth, expecting his quick-fire response. Beyond the open window the air is unseasonal, riffles the fresh concrete of Falkner Place.

She scans the courtyard. Hears the bins tumble again. No one about.

She hesitates, waits. It's over, everyone said. So there's no reason to –

Bernadette bends to her washing-up bowl; she smiles and scrubs two mugs. Brian presented them yesterday, wrapped in a Lewis's bag. He's done odd jobs this summer, cash only, and no, she didn't ask how he –

'Posh cups for a posh new place, Mam,' he'd said, dead proud, cinnamon skin in the summer sunlight, forehead shiny and lips stretched wide. They'd had a toast – he was underage but who cares? Brian, he'll be fifteen in a month, almost a

29

man. Bernadette, she had let the alcohol brand her throat, toasting the hope that bubbled all week.

Last night, late home from Mass, it was only on their return they'd heard –

Bernadette places the mugs on the drainer.

'*Blacks lover!*'

She jerks her head as a bottle hurtles through the kitchen window, skimming her shoulder where the dishcloth words flowed, then a second, broken and slicing her cheek so fast there's blood, hand to skin, oh God, what the –

The missiles hit the linoleum, soft thuds, but now a brick, the brutal wholeness of it smashing the window pane, like the shock of a custard cream lobbed into tea, and them new mugs, they're in bits all over the floor.

She's running, scared, into the hall 'Brian!' and then the lounge 'Brian!' and she's at the front door, shooting the lock, shoving up a table, oh she's scared 'Brian! Brian!' and massed voices, unfamiliar and frantic, join a missile as it hits the porch, and she's scrambling up the stairs, near-slipping on the nylon carpet, 'Salmon Sunset' the council called it, and 'Brian! Where are you? I thought you were –'

But Brian isn't in his room.

Bernadette slams her own door, crouches below the mattressline, kneels in prayer position: 'Hail Mary, full of Grace. The Lord is with thee. Blessed art though among women . . .'

'*Blacks out! Blacks out!*'

Another brick catches the only picture she's hung, Da smiling in his Mod suit way back when, and more's the pity, now he's gone to Heaven –

'Bri-an!'

This time a sharp wail but her son doesn't hear because he's –

Brian sucks tight on the ciggie, returns it to Ruben. He checks his watch, knows Mam will be waiting, tea cooking and TV on, new lounge at the ready.

'This wind, freaks me out. Trouble brewing tonight,' Ruben says. 'I *said* –'

He stops. They both hear bins tumbling. Brian stares at Ruben's profile; sees the undulation of his Afro, a life of its own, bobbing in the breeze.

'Thought it was over – last night?' Brian says.

Ruben flicks ash to concrete, his mustard flares tightening as he leans forward on the step, the slippery fabric glowing in the dusk. Catches Brian's eye.

'I got a knife.' He waits. 'You should too. Tool up, in case.'

'No way.'

'Chicken.' Ruben says it, but kindly, though. 'Nah, keep away, you're too young.'

A knife? Brian thinks of Monday this week, the day he and Mam unpacked in the new kitchen, rehoused and high on the glory of it, slipping their cutlery into a clean drawer, segments for implements, knives and all. 'La-di-da!' he'd said, and she'd turned up Radio City and twisted her hips to Alice Cooper in the charts.

'School's out for summer, school's out forever . . .'

'School's been blown to pieces . . .' he'd sang back, twirling Mam.

He's grown taller than her this summer.

So they danced, him in his Y-fronts and T-shirt and her in

a pinny, getting the place 'shipshape'. That morning, there'd been bacon and eggs on the fancy cooker.

It was ace.

Brian is still thinking this as a bottle smashes at their feet. Ruben is up, quicksilver sharp, and he and Tram and Dave move as one off the step and in slow motion to the street corner, and Brian, he's solo, creeping behind. He sees a phalanx of skinheads shifting forward, twenty of them, it's hard to tell, arms aloft, speeding up, sticks and bottles, and their mouths are open and –

'*Blacks out! Blacks out!*' they're yelling.

The refrain funnels through the Toxteth streets.

Brian wishes he were home with Mam, watching *It's Lulu* on TV, but now he –

No telephone. Bernadette isn't sure where the nearest call box is – and how would she get to it? Running feet crack past her back door; bricks crash other people's walls. Her heart is stomping.

'Hail Mary, full of Grace –'

She thinks of Mammy, silver hair cut neat to the nape, the mother who took her to Mass every Sunday and twice midweek, back in the Belfast days when Bernadette was growing up. And Da, too, who passed away Easter Sunday doing his best to make peace with God. After the Troubles came, who wouldn't at least try?

Bernadette, she was long gone to Liverpool by then.

Stanley, all 6' 4" glory of him, shimmies into her thoughts.

No, she won't think of him –

Bastard.

And yet –

Bernadette gives up with Mary, whispers her boy's name.
'Brian –'

She crawls to peep from the bedroom window, sees them white youths retreating – she knows it's the skinheads, they came last night, everyone said it – and the black boys are chasing, giving as good as they got. Fighting is an evil sound. She hates it, because –

Her eyes scour the tumbling bodies for Brian, but he's nowhere in the mass.

Mess.

She only wants him safe.

Brian makes it home as the scuffling reaches its peak. Doesn't look back.

Lulu; as he watches the pop star, he thinks she's never sounded so good –

Late Sunday, Ruben hands Brian a blade, open palms glistening with sweat.

'Don't be a div. I don't want no fucking knife!'

Brian pushes it away. What he wants is the toilet – fear twirls like a girl in his guts, and he's eyeing the street beyond Falkner Place. Ruben had insisted on his presence. He said: 'Safety in numbers' and 'Blacks stick together, man'. Tonight, there's Tram and Dave and Jamari and more, stalking the four courtyard entrances, eyes strained to the Windsor Gardens Estate, because that's where they'll come from – just like last night and Friday, and the months, on and off, since the spring.

'The Bother', it's been going on this long –

Ruben uses firm fingers to press Brian to sitting.

'So get your own knife, Soul Boy.' His jaw tightens.

'Blacks fight as one.'

Brian squeezes shut his eyes, pictures Mam. She's not black: creamy Irish skin, splintering emerald eyes, the full cliché. Mam is beautiful when she's not tired from working shifts. Dad steps into his head, too – swinging Brian round their previous crowded flat, the occasional ride on the Ferry-Cross-the-Mersey, churning wind whipping their cheeks, but the memory is fuzzy. Unlike Dad's silhouette as he left for good, way back, running away –

'Coward!' Mam had screamed. 'Stand up, tell the truth!'

Brian and Mam, they've been a team for years.

Ruben ain't sitting. Him and the others, they've dragged wood, combing the slum clearances around Upper Parliament Street for spoils and makeshift armour. They've nailed front doors, piled bricks and boxes at the courtyard entrances. Brian sees Tram has two knives. They sparkle as he slips them from view, into his waistband.

They wait for the white boys to come. Feels like hours, but it's minutes.

Brian longs to pee. He wants –

He *wishes* he were curled in Mam's lap, seven again and sucking sherbet fountain.

Ruben says, low: 'The lads are on their way from Granby. Won't be long.'

A solid boulder arcs the courtyard wall. Where's the backup? Brian thinks.

He pukes in the corner, splashes his C&A jeans. Mam will be furious.

Acute silence.

Everyone's waiting before the attack. Brian peers between shoulders, sees the skinheads coming, a diaphanous blue-black mirage, denim jackets and bovver boots and white puckered faces. They stop to narrow the group, round it to a solid contour, tight with spin, ready to bounce. Ten, nine, eight, seven, six . . . Brian counts and –

Then the roar, and the lads – no, they're men, brawn and tight jaws, broad shoulders, crowning Afros – are streaming round the corner from Brian's old street, so *they're* the backup, and boom, those skinny-arsed white boys, they've a fight on their hands.

Ruben grips a bottle, holds it aloft. He's sixteen, seems brave as hell, and yet –

Brian sees Ruben's long fingers tremble. The same fingers that play acoustic guitar, soft and sweet, in his bedroom, when Brian comes over and they hang out, talking crazy shit and dreaming big. The hands that cradle Brian's pet mouse –

Ruben says: 'Always told Bernadette I'd take care of you. So piss off home.'

Thankful, doubling back to number 16, Brian wants to sprint. But running looks guilty and draws attention, he's learned that much. The fighting has eddied the width of the street; the courtyard is emptying. He imagines the mams and sisters, nanas and friends, hiding behind bolted doors, kids whimpering at their knees. Diagonally opposite, a police jeep screeches, but them coppers, they don't get out. A woman, all tight ponytail and drooping shoulders, she heads towards the policeman's window, shouting loud.

Any moment, the bizzies will spill out, stop this fighting, Brian thinks.

The police, surely – aren't they here to protect?

But the woman is walking away. Shoos at him with a

frantic hand.

'Go inside, lad. They ain't getting out. They're doing sod all. Too scared.'

At number 16, he's sure Mam is waiting but Brian's legs are jelly. Forces himself, even so, to be the man, to say it first –

'You OK, Mam? I'm here.'

They stand in the hall, light barely piercing the wood shutter Ruben hammered earlier, over the side window, to assist Bernadette.

Brian can't help that he pees on the floor, no warning, face flaming.

Mam wipes it up. 'Get the kettle on, Brian.'

It's only after, drinking tea from chipped mugs, away from the windows, that they realise they're shivering. Brian puts hands to his ears, can't bear the smudging horror of shouts and sirens. Mam, too.

The stray dogs, Alsatians mostly, barking fit to burst.

Come Monday, everyone's full of last night. From her kitchen, Bernadette sees the women clustering front doors. Some she recognises from Granby where they used to live; some she doesn't. She likes that they're white, mixed race, black. Ever since she met Stanley (English born, Jamaican dad and mum, sexy as hell – how could she resist?) she's not minded. Who cares? Brian, mixed race, she's raised him not to see the *colour* of his mates' skins but 'See what's in their hearts, Brian.'

She thinks she's succeeded. He's a good boy.

He hangs out sometimes with Billy – Maria's son, from church – and *he's* white.

Last night, after the fighting died away, she'd tossed and turned restlessly, fizzing sparks between the nylon sheets. Three times she rose to check Brian was still in bed, not lured away. She trusts Ruben; he's two years Brian's senior, has always looked out for him. Almost a father figure now Stanley isn't around. *Loves* him, she thinks.

Even so, she –

At four a.m. she'd found herself on the landing, leaning into the bedroom meant for Mammy.

The rehousing from their condemned tenement had come too late for her.

Bernadette's eyes filled with tears. Them councillors. Them bastards –

Too bad Mammy died this spring, May 1972.

The small room is empty; they've barely any furniture. 'Box room', that's what the Victorians would have called it. Bernadette knows. She devours every nineteenth-century novel she can lay her hands on, always has. On the bus, exhausted, to and from the car factory. At night in bed, for a few minutes until sleep claims her. Mammy said, that day Bernadette called from a phone box, pregnant and hitched to Stanley, crimson with shame –

'University! All wasted. Say your Hail Marys, Bernadette.'

After his Monday tea, Brian lingers, tells Mam he's putting up rock 'n' roll posters. He's playing music in his room; bought a new single with the money from Mr Lawrence's Most Improved Performance prize. (Their TV, his record player, they were both his Irish grandma's doing. A brown envelope, stuffed with cash 'to be spent on fun', she'd written before she died. 'God love her,' Mam said.)

He hopes not to hear Ruben's low whistle beneath his bedroom window. But of course he does, and he jumps, can't afford not to go; he must keep face with the lads. Leaves *Popcorn* by Hot Butter on repeat, trusts the record player to take the strain.

Ruben, Tram and Jamari are waiting. Their arms are looped through those of older lads, silver chains bouncing at open necks, chest hair coiled. Brian swaggers in, sniffs the air; it stinks of fear and chips, leaks into his lungs.

'Hey, Soul Boy. Got that knife? Remember, I told you,' Ruben warns.

A man is talking. He's from the Jungle, what they call where Brian used to live. Blacks, mainly. This guy's muscles bulge his shirtsleeves. Brian can't meet his eye.

'All right lads, we're ready – there's fifty of us, it won't take long.'

Brian says to Ruben: 'Don't want no trouble. Here – take it, take the knife.'

Ruben puts out a hand, reaches for the handle, barely visible, and then grasps it. Brian feels the warmth of Ruben's fingers touching his waistband; they stay there one second too long.

Brian cracks his knuckles. Says nothing. Wishes he were with Billy instead.

'None of this would be happening if we had jobs.'

Jamari says it but they all murmur 'Yeah.'

And it's true. White, black, mixed – they've all left school, and there's no work. Brian knows Ruben has been unemployed since he left the comp last summer; he helps his Dad fix burnt-out cars but it isn't a real –

Brian has another two years to study, can't leave until he's sixteen. Tonight, facing trouble, even the iron stare of Mr Matthews, that bastard headmaster, seems inviting. After these skirmishes, the enclosed tarmac playground will seem like Paradise. He and Billy, they play footie most breaktimes, smoke around the back.

'Come on, white boys, show your faces,' Ruben says.

'Fuck yeah,' Brian says, pushing thoughts of Billy away.

(Mam wasn't looking when he took the kitchen knife earlier, slid it into his waistband, like he'd seen Ruben do.)

Ruben, he fixes Brian with cocoa eyes; they're glittering, all fear gone.

'You're one of us, Brian, like it or not.'

He teases a curl from Brian's forehead; gentle touch. Sometimes, Brian thinks Ruben looks at him too long, too close. His gaze is scorching, barely inches away.

'Cut your hair short as you like, but look at your spread nose, lad, them lips –'

(Ruben didn't see Brian, hours earlier, before he left the house. While Mam was washing up, he slipped into her bedroom. Didn't take long to find her compact, work Crème Puff into his dusky skin. He put on a hat. Who would know, in the failing light, with the powder and hat and all, if he's black or white or in between?)

Brian thinks he's both and neither.

Surely – if them skinheads target anyone, it ain't going to be him?

Bernadette sits in the lounge. She's nervous but Ruben has said she'll be secure. After tonight, it'll peter out, he promised. Brian has stayed home; she's 'had a word'. He's in his room, the door's shut, OK, she knows what fourteen-year-old boys get up to but at least he's out of trouble.

They've hardboard on the back door, a chair against the front.

Them police have done nothing.

She thinks of Maria, she's on the Windsor Gardens Estate, her and Billy and the baby. Bernadette isn't sure what this fighting will do to their friendship. Maria visited just last week, brought a house-warming gift: 'I bought it in the sale! From Blacklers!'

Her eyes, they slid across the new rooms like fire melting butter.

Bernadette lets out a steady sigh. They've eaten tea early. She settles away from the window, picks up *Middlemarch*. She believes there's solace in history and literature.

For all the bad things he's done, she wishes (just tonight) Stanley were here. Of course, he'd be out with the Granby lads, in the thick of things, protecting her, but causing trouble too –

Brian, he's not like that. He'd do anything for a quiet life, wouldn't hurt a fly. He just needs a nice ordinary girl, Irish maybe, or Jamaican, she doesn't care which way he goes, what colour, just for him to be happy, and that'll be that –

She sighs, drops her eyes to the open page.

What would Dorothea do tonight? What would she say?

Bernadette buries her nose deep in the book; it's from the library and smells of other people's fingers, but she doesn't care.

Brian's been sitting behind the makeshift barricades with Ruben and massed others. There's the stink of BO and countless fags. Tension in the air, he could light it with a match. The sky is stretched to a purple bruise –

'They're coming!'

It's not Ruben; Brian doesn't recognise the voice, it's rough-edged and strange, but they all hear it. The group moves precisely from sitting to standing, first tentatively and then stopping, feet firmly planted, muscles tense, jaws tight. Brian rocks with fresh terror. He's glad he passed that carving knife to Ruben; he don't want no trouble.

'*Blacks out! Blacks out!*'

The first shock of a brick and now thirty to forty skinheads are scattering the road, piercing the courtyard. Brian, surrounded by his black neighbours, feels the rush of comradeship. On balance, this is better, good, the best.

'*Black power! Black power!*'

Soon he's chanting with all the rest.

The barrier crashes over and the skinheads are onto them fighting and Brian is at the centre but he's nothing to scrap with and –

Sat in the police patrol jeep, two streets from the fray, PC Stuart Hedges pictures his wife's ripe belly, can almost feel its contours tingling the palm of his sweaty hand. PC Andy Dowell coughs in the passenger seat.

'Getting closer.'

PC Dowell cranes his head down Upper Parliament Street; night is coming and it's hard to get a dekko. In the distance, there are shouts and crashes and the car is filled with endless radio fuzz. PC Hedges cracks his attention to the here and now, where he doesn't want to be.

'We going in then?'

'Be ready.'

PC Hedges is glad of the height and solidity of their jeep, the truncheon in his hand and the riot gear if required. It's the fourth night of rioting, only his second on duty. Janie had circled her arms around him as he left, planted a soft kiss.

'Take care, love, me and the baby need you.'

He's taking care, love, make no mistake. He's grateful for being two streets away, that he's not one of the coppers already out, home-made petrol bombs scraping the air, and the blacks and whites clobbering the hell out of each other.

He exhales a low, stressed sigh. Only started six months ago.

'Tell me again, Andy,' he says. 'Explain it. Need to know.'

PC Dowell spits it out, a textbook passage learned by heart.

'They've rehoused mixed families – some from the tenements in Granby – into this new estate, Falkner Place. The whites in Windsor Gardens don't like it, they're jealous. Youth clubs are closed for summer – the black lads ain't got no work, the white lads neither. It's a tinder box.' He turns his head to meet PC Hedges' eyes. 'And what d'you expect?' he asks. 'The blacks hate the whites and think we favour them. The whites hate the blacks and also think we favour them. They want to beat the shit out of each other, and they hate us, too. Want to know the answer?'

'Yep.'

'Jobs. Proper employment. It's a start –'

He stretches out his legs and the radio barks.

'Backup, backup!'

Without speaking, PC Hedges puts his foot on the accelerator and they're off, down Upper Parliament Street, on to Falkner Place, everywhere roving bodies, it's almost too dark to distinguish what colour skin, and who cares? PC Dowell leans into the back of the jeep, reaching for his riot shield.

'Going in?'

PC Hedges thinks of his baby, patiently waiting to be born. He doesn't know if it's a girl or a boy, but he needs it now, soft and mewling in his lap. Doesn't want to be here, his face aglow with a dozen skirmish fires and the yowling of dogs and boys and angry men.

'Get your gear on.'

It's a command from PC Dowell, and PC Hedges understands the urgency: he reaches for the equipment, then turns to see a brick winging through the windscreen, and in slow motion he's thinking of Janie in hospital, sees her labouring without him in that split second before its contact with PC Andy Dowell, and now his fellow copper is down, head lolling on his shoulder, blood spilling, the motor still running and a black kid, close – too close, arm still aloft –

'Shit, shit, shit . . .'

He jams the accelerator and does a U-turn, speeds off in the opposite direction, there's no point calling for backup.

Because they *are* the backup, already deployed –

Early on, Billy was at the ragged tail of the mob; now he's running fit to burst, up front. He's had five beers and Kev insisted on another. Tonight's the night, they've agreed, and they'll knock out them black kids from the Jungle. He told his mum he was going to fight and she only turned away, exhausted, the baby on her shoulder, and slowly said: 'What would your dad say if he was alive?'

He's heard it before. Thing is, money's tight and the baby's sick.

He's not having them blacks taking new flats, rightfully theirs.

Across the sea of anonymous faces, jiggling in the dusk, he spies Brian. Billy didn't want to clock anyone familiar, makes things difficult. He's no bone to pick with Brian; they were mates long before school bound them. And what the hell is he doing here anyway? Brian is the gentlest boy in class. Billy likes him, doesn't care what colour he is, and yet – what's he doing with the –

'*Blacks out! Blacks out!*'

He joins in the shout, presses on. Next to Brian he sees that bastard Ruben, he's been here every night, a troublemaker, thinks he's tough, but he's not, he's a –

Billy, he raises his brick, but he's so drunk and pumped his aim is wobbly. He angles away from Brian, chucks it straight at Ruben –

But something happens. In the thick of it, the brick swerves, and it's shooting instead straight at Brian. Billy sees Ruben clock it, and Ruben shoves Brian out the way, takes the hit himself, hard on the shoulder, but it doesn't stop him, he only speeds up. Billy sees as Ruben lunges, a kitchen knife in his hand, and Billy looks down, thinks, He's got me, a searing surprise as the blade ripples into his flesh and soon he's –

Brian sees Ruben jab at Billy, so close there's blood sprayed on his jeans. He's caught out: he knows Ruben did it for him, understands the game is up, he's tangled in something he wants no part of but it's too late now. Another white guy is coming straight at Ruben, knife out, and Ruben is jeering, hands wide, saying: 'Come on, skinny white boy – I dare you!' but the problem is, that white boy, Kev, he does dare, and now Ruben is down too –

Brian knows he should be fighting with his brothers, but he can't decide which side he's on – because he's black or he's white or he's –

He pictures Bernadette, kneeling by her bed, saying her desperate Hail Marys. Home, he needs to get home. He slows his pace, walks backwards away from the running battles, head down, moves diagonally and shy of the bizzies, muscling in with riot shields and shouts, and he hears the scream of ambulances, and are they coming for Billy, or Ruben, or –

Bernadette is shut in the bathroom; she's jammed the door. She's reading *Middlemarch*, and she's put herself in a dream world, where nothing matters but what Dorothea does next. The sounds of rioting fill her with terror. Her younger brother, Declan, that's how he died, three years back on the streets in Belfast, when the Troubles got going. She has fingers pressed deep in her ears.

Even so, she still hears Brian's banging, and she's half running, half slipping down the stairs, that damn Salmon Sunset will be the death of her. She drags Brian in, but this time he doesn't smile.

'Going to my room, Mam.'

'You've something on your jeans, you've –'

Her fingers touch the dampness, come away scarlet.

'What have you done, Brian?' Shakes him by the shoulders.

'Nothin' . . .'

'Are you telling me the truth, Brian?'

'Nothin'!'

Brian turns away. Slams his bedroom door. Puts a record on the turntable and turns up the volume so loud the room shakes. The electric sounds of Hot Butter on repeat explode like teardrops and he's crying too. He saw the whites of Ruben's eyes as he fell senseless to the ground.

Next morning, the police are everywhere but nowhere; they're not helping the residents at Falkner Place. 'And that's for sure,' says Mam. 'Stay inside, Brian.'

No whistle as usual from Ruben below Brian's window.

Brian waits while Mam makes him toast in the kitchen, then she drags him to the table, takes both his hands. Today her face is white as soap. His skin, next to hers, is dusky brown. The colour of the coffee she's made, stirring in the powdered milk.

'Ruben said it would blow over,' Mam says. 'Let's hope that's it.'

Outside, there's the bellow of someone at the door. Engines running.

Brian sits at the table, watches his mam walk into the hall and open up.

'Mrs Grant?'

He sees Mam lean on the lintel. Today the sky is almond pale, the wind has dropped and there's a patch of sunlight on the carpet. He imagines him and Mam, in two years' time, he'll be studying for A levels or have an apprenticeship. This new house, it's a promise to them both. He and Mam will get rich and one day they'll move out to somewhere posher, Aigburth or Mossley Hill –

Ruben's face swims into view. So does Billy's. Brian wants to pee, real bad.

He hears the policeman asking –

'You're asking – where is my kitchen knife?'

Bernadette stares straight at PC Hedges with confusion in her heart and clarity in her head. She's still leaning on the lintel; she'll maintain this relaxed posture if it's the last thing she does. Beyond the copper's shoulders, she sees the jeep is full of plain-clothes policemen, thick necks, piercing eyes, three abreast in the back.

'Yes, Mrs Grant. We need to see your kitchen knife.'

'And you are?'

'My name is PC Hedges. One of our officers was injured last night. There's a teenage boy, fighting for his life at the hospital. A man stabbed to death. So you'll understand why we –'

Bernadette is thinking of the house-warming gift Maria brought. She'd stood in the kitchen, passed it over, red handle, smart as anything – she'd given Bernadette a kiss. Eyes a little jealous. 'So fresh here!' She'd paused. 'Give us a penny – bad luck otherwise, knives as presents.'

Bernadette had felt in her pocket.

'It's payday two weeks Monday. Pay you back then?'

Oh, how she wishes it had been sooner. Maria never got her penny and so –

'Show me the knife, Mrs Grant.'

Bernadette turns on her heel, slippery sharp, leads the way. She already knows there's a gap in the cutlery drawer.

She's known it, without understanding why.

The copper is bulking the kitchen, right behind her, and

Brian sits on.

'The white boy who was stabbed – it was a kitchen knife, red-handled type, recovered. The boy's mother, Maria, she's identified it as . . .'

Bernadette's heart is cantering as she pulls open the kitchen drawer –

Brian understands everything in a crystalline moment.

Ruben is dead. Billy is fighting for his life.

The kitchen knife Ruben used – they will think, everyone will think –

PC Hedges and the boy's mother peer into the drawer. PC Hedges' son arrived prematurely last night; he's already held him. Oh the joy! But PC Dowell is in intensive care. And this little bastard, Brian, there's no doubt in PC Hedges' mind –

'I don't understand,' Bernadette whispers.

The back door is open and –

'No, Brian!' *Don't run away.* 'Tell them the truth!' she screams.

Outside, bins tumble. Bernadette prays. Seconds, minutes, and –

Brian walks back into the kitchen. Bernadette's heart swells.

'Got kids, PC Hedges?' she asks, firm hands on Brian's shoulders. The copper looks exhausted.

'A baby.' He smiles, like sun dawning. 'Last night – a son.'

'You'll be needing tea, then?' she says. 'Parenthood. It's precious.'

48

She turns to Brian. *She'll make this work.*

'Now the truth, lad,' she says, fixing her gaze on PC Hedges. 'Because this man, he's a proud new dad. He's listening.'

PC Hedges nods.

'I'm listening, Brian,' he says.

The Girls

Isha Karki

We are five when I see her across the playground. She's wearing a yellow raincoat just like mine – 'Daffodils against mud,' Mama said that morning, licking her thumb and smudging the dirt on my cheek.

Last week, when we finally went to the shops like Mama promised, I spent ages smoothing lambswool and velvet and kidskin between my fingers. The raincoat, tucked behind huge puffed jackets, was waxy. It drew me in and repulsed me. I rubbed my hands over its surface. Mama, rolling her eyes, reached to find the price tag buried within. When we got to the counter, the old woman, lipstick smeared at the corners of her mouth, said, 'Aren't we a lucky girl? We only have two left in this colour. Best snap it right up.'

Mama always makes us late but on that first day, we skip breakfast and she forgets my lunch, so we get there five minutes early. The air is crisp, singed faintly with woodsmoke. That year, the leaves turned early, wildfire catching tree to tree, so when we get to the squat building, the copse in front seems a trembling pyre. A throng of coats cluster the playground just beyond, bodies gravitating towards one another amidst rising chatter. There's a tangle in my stomach; I imagine it to be coarse and unyielding like wheat-coloured rope. Mama's hand is crushing mine, and I want to tug it away, but I know she won't like it.

Instead, I look at the backs of the children's heads, tilted towards each other, the hoods of their coats, pulled up. None of their faces are visible, and suddenly it seems to me they are all faceless, scrubbed of foreheads, cheeks and chins –

The girl in the yellow raincoat turns to me.

She has a kothi on her lip, exactly where mine sits; a layer of spun sugar crusts the skin above her mouth. I swipe my nose and what is leaking from hers appears on the back of my hand. She looks like me, glimpsed through water. When we come to know one another, I will see that one nose is a fraction wider, one pair of eyelashes more curled, one head of hair glossier and one set of lips plumper, parted by slightly protruding teeth. One of us also has a dimple so deep you could slot a whole coin into it – or a key.

In that moment, when she is the only one turned towards me, I want – even then – to know the texture of her skin, to know how it might feel smoothed on top of my own, the way Mama smoothed leathers and furs over her arms.

A few days later, Mama and I will return to the store to buy boots and I will see the other raincoat, buttons done up wrong, a shoulder slipping off the hanger. But right then, I am certain the girl wears the last yellow raincoat and *aren't we lucky, we only have two left in this colour* that we will be Best Friends forever.

That's the first night I remember my dream.

I am eating, in the way my grandmother did as her body waited to crumble to ash. I gather the food with my hand and place it in the wet O of my mouth. The thali in front of me is large; while I chew, my fingers rest on battered copper, skin turned white and stiff.

I plunge my hand into the steaming pile; the meat pulses, almost alive. I swallow another mouthful and my stomach strains like it might if you drank a litre of seawater, then another and another.

Mama appears in front of me, and I become aware of my face smeared with viscous liquid. Her gaze is sharp, body held strangely, as if any minute, her arm will dart out and –

What are you eating?

We slot into each other's days. We share lunches, rectangles of bread layered with ham and cheese, cartons of apple juice, straws nibbled by one set of teeth and felt by the tongue of another, cookies precisely broken and consumed in halves; the tear of clementine pieces counted into palms; the snap of a KitKat. Her mother packs us laddu and pakora in paper that crinkles and glistens with grease. Her father sends us film cases stuffed with cashews, walnuts, dried raisins and misri that look like crystals found inside trunks in the attic.

In the afternoons, our stomachs growl, one lunch never enough for two.

When asked to read aloud in class, we applaud each other, even if the words turn upside down and knock against our teeth. When one of us is desperate for the bathroom and told to wait, something hot dribbles from both our seats, a shared rush of relief, pools of golden light merging, chairs clattering across the classroom as other children recoil.

53

The second time Ruby Wright sneaks in a bundle in her bag and rubs her baby brother's soiled diaper on the back of my head shrieking, 'Foundation for your shit-coloured skin', and it splits open, I am left heaving from the stench. My Best Friend – the taller, braver one – barrels into her. We hear bone striking wood. A spray of blood; rubies glistering on my shoes. A teacher's booming voice. Sylvie Wane, Ruby's Best Friend – with ribbons in her hair and a nose bent just like Ruby's – is screaming and screaming.

My Best Friend's violence, on my behalf, fills me: that wheat-coloured knot bloating within. I could never have done it, I think, and that is perhaps the first clear thought I remember.

Years later, I ask Mama about her Best Friend. 'Did you have one?'

Her hands pause over the blooms, the way they do when she spots a thorn. 'Of course.'

'How come I haven't met her?'

Mama snips the stems. Sometimes, she's so single-minded she switches the lights off when I'm still in the room. Even when I call out, she doesn't realise her mistake. One of my earliest memories is of distress, perhaps I'd lost a toy or scraped my knees or was almost stolen away by a stranger; I was tugging at Mama's kurthi, cotton coarse in my hands, and she didn't turn to me once.

The sound of scissors gripping stems, then slicing, fills the silence. A sharp green smell seeps out of the cuts. Packets of plant food lay strewn across the counter; one is pierced and solution bubbles from the hole. Mama will discard these. *They must learn to fend for themselves. Otherwise, they'll fatten and rot too soon.*

'Have I met her?' I ask, hesitation creeping into my voice. I search through smudges of memory and discover a weightier shadow next to Mama. Perhaps I had met Mama's Best Friend and age scrubbed the image away. I try again: 'How come we don't see her any more?'

'Oh.' Mama's words are a sigh. A cool wind blows in just then, and a leaf, come loose, clings to the sap on her fingers. 'She's here.'

In high school, we rush to each other's house as soon as it's half three, and just before six, we settle on the sofa with a bowl of jhalmuri, two spoons stuck into the mixture, eyes fixed on the boxy TV with its five channels. We transport ourselves to Summer Bay with its twins who, hundreds of episodes on, find out they aren't twins at all. One of us bites green chilli and we both cry out from the sudden burn. We hold halved samosas in one hand and enraptured by Kim Hyde, sensing the almost-there outline of the divine body he will grow into, our mouths part and hands tilt. The aloo falls out, a hot dollop on our crotch, leaving only the husk of pastry behind.

One sleepover, someone chooses a horror film. We watch a creature rip through the woman's womb, its limbs made of things that shred and slice, dripping with a tar-like substance that surely couldn't have come from her.

That night, we curl around each other, cocooned under the duvet, something roiling beneath our stomach. When I dream, it's the same dream: my mother flinging the door open – *What are you eating?* – and my hand plunged into meat, coated in a viscous substance that has perhaps come from inside my own body after all.

A few days later, Ms Underwood calls on her in our PSHE Future Dreams class and my Best Friend announces, 'I want twin babies.' A shudder runs through my body with such violence she leans away from me.

I think, with still-water clarity, I could never do that – and it is the second thought I remember, unpeeled from my Best Friend's mind.

Otherwise, we are two brown faces on a white-pebbled beach – though one of us is lighter-skinned than the other – and even the teachers tell us we could be identical. We don't ever tire of hearing it; we sit up straighter, place our hands demurely in front of us and smile just so. We've outgrown the yellow raincoat, but though we've shed that skin, we find we can borrow one another's. We tell no one how I slip my hand into her mother's at home time, sit in her chair, eat hot paratha with a scoop of ghee, laugh at Bollywood comedies, and sleep in her bed after gulping down a cup of honey-swirled milk, stomach swelling from intolerance.

One night, I am missing Best Friend's sure-bodied presence next to me, so I call out to Mama. She appears, illuminated by the corridor light. 'Yes?'

'Do you think we were swapped at birth?'

There's a strange expression on Mama's face. After a while, she says, 'You could've been.'

Then, one day, Mr Goodfellow asks one of us to help prepare for Parents' Evening, and by the time the meeting is over, there's only fifteen minutes left of lunch, and when we get to the canteen, one of us is surrounded by other girls, laughter spilling through the gaps of a tight circle.

In the mornings, our timing is off, one of us already seated in a far corner of the classroom.

'Hey,' we say, as bags thump on the ground around us, phones brandished, and weekend antics relayed.

'Early today?'

'Yep, came by car.'

'Really? How come?'

A brief moment of hesitation, then: 'One of the triple science girls picked me up.'

One of us starts leaving earlier, straight after history or maths, without mentioning it. Lunchtimes, we have library duty or a prefect meeting or a mock exam or a revision session, and when we emerge, there is the ring of girls again.

At weekends, we still cram into the alcove seat at our local Starbucks.

'Did you finish the essay?'

'Yes,' we say. 'Did you?'

'I couldn't.'

'Do you need help?'

We shake our head.

'This topic is going to be on the exam – I can feel it.'

'What does it feel like?' There's a small smile on our face, the old smile.

'Sticky.'

We slurp iced coffees, one of us scrolling through Instagram on a new phone with a glittery cover that catches sunlight and scatters it into people's eyes. Our drinks are at the same level; if someone were to pop the lid off, upend the contents, and count the ice cubes, it would be the same number, edges melted to the exact degree.

A man passes us, pushing a buggy, and its handle knocks

against our table. One of the coffees tips to its side.

'*Shit.*'

We grab tissues to mop it up and our movements are suddenly uncoordinated, soggy paper dabbed on each other's hands, brown liquid dripping onto white sneakers. The other coffee stands, untouched.

The year we both flower, as Mama calls it, we have one of the last sleepovers. Bellies stuffed with Strawbs and popcorn, M&M's peanuts stuck on our teeth, we spend hours watching *Charmed* on a flat wide screen, moving only to change the disc. We don't talk about the Deputy Head sacked because of a sixth former we know, or about our form teacher sneaking out for cigarettes and coming back red-eyed because of a break-up, or about the boy who's been sending us messages every evening for the past two weeks. We just watch the first season, till the last episode where time is rewound again and again to the same moment – till it isn't – then sleep on separate beds. One is a mattress on the floor. In the dark, we are at different heights; our backs curve away from one another.

That year, one of us gets to fuck the cool guy in the year above, on a bed so low, when he pushes us onto it, it feels like falling from a tall building, and the rush of it, the flash of fear, feels like desire. We don't talk about it – even though the need to ask questions is like a creature waiting to burst out of our bodies.

That year, there are no more midnight snacks or lunch trips to McDonald's or lazy days chopping ingredients. Instead, one of us gets to fuck the cool guy in the year above and stops eating – though we don't ever speak of it – and one of us, somehow, after a party and the first taste of tequila and a smoky haze of missed calls and missed buses, ends up having a different kind of story.

But suddenly, it's everywhere. The story of the car and the man, of the park and the man, and everyone laughs and doesn't once think it's anything more than a funny story. Rumours swirl about the girl with blowjob lips who gives head for car rides and the rumour, the burning shame of it, the way it strips all power, means we can't bear to look at each other. Because if we do, we see the dimple and a key slotted in and secrets spilling out and we remember tears hot in our eyes the time my knees scraped raw against stones and dirt, the hand gripping my hair so tight, and his dick ramming and bulging inside my throat.

The twist of the key: I could never forgive that. That is the third thought.

One day, Mama stares at me as I spoon cereal into my mouth, almond milk rolling on my tongue, sweet and creamy, and says: 'You look different.'

My head, which has been lolling, as if someone is slipping inside my room every night and pouring concrete into my eyes, snaps up. Mama's standing in front of me, shoulders tight, as she does in my dreams, and sure enough the next words out of her mouth are –

'What are you eating?'

When I look up, hands in a Doritos bag, I see Alex Victor, lips curling in what could be a smile. I raise my eyebrows and shake the bag of crisps. I don't offer her any.

'Are you mad?'

'What?'

59

'Are you mad at your Best Friend?'

My hand drops so suddenly on top of the crisp packet, the resulting crunch jars the quiet, and Alex's lips stretch even more. 'Why would I be?'

'I heard she's got a Boyfriend now.'

'So?'

'So, everyone knows he liked you first. You can talk to me if you want.'

A scene from a few years ago flashes into my mind: two girls rolling around the frozen mud during PE, clawing at each other, the rest of us screeching and gasping. Alex was the one who'd emerged from the tangle of limbs first.

I also remember that Alex Victor's Best Friend has been missing for three weeks. People say she was seen getting into a van with a stranger, that she's locked up in some grown man's basement, that she simply started disappearing one day at school, the sun shining through her translucent flesh, then organs, then bone, till nothing of her could be seen.

'You know,' Alex says, sitting down next to me, the mint of her chewing gum a cool sensation on my face, 'that's how it is with Best Friends. Only one of you –'

I don't know what she says next because when she places her hand on the table beside me, her pinky touches mine. An electric charge runs up my arm. I snatch my hand away.

The summer that one of us goes on the pill, skin lumping and breaking into a scatter of spots, one of us begins to move differently.

My body knocks against doorframes. I get stuck trying to pass the ticket barriers at train stations. When I walk, parts of me slam into bike handles, sweep lunch trays off canteen tables, and push people into oncoming traffic. The startled honks of cars and shouts of mothers follow me around. It's as if I've forgotten my own dimensions, slipped back to a prelapsarian stage where space and solidity mean nothing.

Every night, I dream I am meticulously cutting up meat with knife and fork that have the heft of hammers. When I'm done, I fling them away and dig in with both hands, tearing flesh from bone, sucking on marrow so it slides rich and heavy down my throat. I eat and eat and eat and, slowly, something oozes out of the seams of my stomach.

The PE teacher notices bruises in strange places on my body and calls to ask if everything is fine. Mama rolls her eyes and says, 'She's just getting fat and clumsy,' but promises to take me to the doctor's. At the surgery, they plunge a long needle into my arm and draw a vial full of blood and I pee into a slim plastic tube, two drops landing perfectly on the back of my hand. I don't tell them how taut my breasts are or how my back aches even when I'm flat on the bed.

The results come back. That summer, one of us gives up the pill and gets the coil, and one of us gets pregnant. There's no memory of the sex that should have come before it, but suddenly there's something alien invading our most secret places. We never discuss it, not once, but we know instinctively that in both cases, it's too late to decide anything different.

'What is it?'

We are sitting next to each other in my room. She has brought two packets of paun with her; just thinking of the dark strips slathered in a sludge of chilli gathers saliva in my mouth. Her mother sent it, she says, but I know my Best

Friend is the one who felt it deep as the craving hit me last night.

She moves her hand to her shirt pocket as if reaching for something, then puts it back on her lap. My own are placed firmly on the bed, braced.

'I got my letter from Oxford.'

Something slackens in me.

'I'm so proud of you.' I turn to hug her – but even that is not the same, a hard bump between us.

'Have you . . . ?' Her voice is muffled in my hair.

I shake my head. I don't tell her I never made the application, that Mama talked to the Head about taking a year or two out of school and the Head clasped Mama's hands, shed a few tears, and offered her tea.

But when my Best Friend leans back, something about the purse of her mouth tells me she *knows*.

My eyes focus on her as if for the first time in years. She is thin, thinner than I ever was, skin stretched over the bones of her face. Everything about her is sharp, as if she has been outlined with black felt tip, once, twice, three times. Next to her, I am a watercolour, dribbling onto the page.

I understand, then, something of what it means to have a Best Friend – and a little more of the thing inside me. I know that when it comes out, it will look more like her than it will ever look like me.

The other thoughts I have as we stare at each other, left corner of her mouth still drawn up, are not real thoughts but an echo: *That's how it is with Best Friends. Only one of you –*

The morning I come home, I finally sleep.

In the hospital, Mama flitted in and out of my room,

blowing noisily on coffee, unwrapping and crunching chocolate bars, fiddling with the remote control, making my bed jerk upright then flat. I gripped the polyester sheets, rough in hands scrubbed with anti-bacterial gel. I said, 'Mama . . .' and she snapped, 'I'm trying to get you comfortable.' Her breath smelt faintly of sick. She left me for hours without a word, and that at least soothed me with its familiarity.

Nurses came at six, ten and two – but that was all. It was exam period, I knew. But in years past, we'd revised intensely and timetabled breaks for movie binges and trips to the shops. Absence filled that tiny room, a giant balloon expanding, and every time it sucked in more air, I was left breathless. The nurses rushed to check my vitals and pressed into my palms tablets whittled into small shapes; I slipped into a drowsiness that kept me from real sleep.

At home, in the seconds before I drift off, I hear myself as I was hours before in the stirrups. Screaming and screaming and sloughing off something once hopeful and yearning –

I sink into the dream.

My fingers are scooping meat into my eager mouth; flecks of black cling to my oiled lips. This time, there is no viscous substance. Instead, the meat is charred and smoking as if it has just been lifted from embers. I drag the largest piece from the mound, fingertips blistering, and chew the hot flesh. Hairline cracks spider across my stomach but I don't stop. I know I will eat it all, meat and bones and even the gristle lodged between my teeth.

Gradually, I become aware of an object to the left of me. I turn towards it. The meat falls from my hand with a soft thud.

I stare at the head, torn from its body, upright on its neck. There's a kothi on its lip just where mine sits. Its eyelashes

63

are curled, hair glossy, lips plump, and it has a dimple so deep an entire key could slot in.

The sudden crash of the thali as I push it away, as far as I can with my greasy hands, is so jarring that I –

My mother lets herself in, the opening of the door startling me awake. She stops, looks first at me, then at the bed. There's a whimper and a stink in the air. Mama goes to the bundle and does something with her fingers. A few seconds later, a shuddering exhalation, as if she has been holding her breath.

She comes to stand in front of me, and when she speaks, her voice quivers like one of her leaves, struggling to balance a drop of rain on its surface: 'Something is wrong with you.'

I don't say anything. But as she looms over me, I think how she must see herself reflected in my pupils, two miniatures, trapped inside her child's body.

I don't hear from my Best Friend.

The summer is ripe, bruised at the edges. In a week or two, her parents, mother draped in a sari, father sporting a flat cap, will pack their car with stacks of books and Tupperware boxes, slotted next to a mini ironing board, a portable hoover, and suitcases stuffed from last-minute shopping sprees. Once, we would have mulled over clothes that might be suitable for formal dinners and sweaty clubs; we would have imagined running to a kebab truck at four a.m. and grabbing hangover espressos the next morning.

I cast my mind back to those secret swaps when I lay next to these same parents. The me in those moments could have had this future: sitting in the back seat, earphones in, tapping freshly painted nails against glass, watching the trees and the houses, the sky and the future, rush towards me.

Our lives will converge every few years.

One Dashain, when my Best Friend comes home, we will meet by chance at the temple. Her parents will reach forward to put tika on my forehead, and she will do the same. The mixture will drip and from afar it will look as if I have been shot in the head, an extra in a low-budget horror, the blood too bright and too red to be real.

I will visit her in college. The dew-studded grounds sweeping around me, the flow of the river, and the peek of a small furry thing through thick brush will move me to tears. She will go out with her friends, asking if I'll be OK to spend the night alone.

I will have no memory of the years in between.

I sit in my bedroom; if I am quiet and imagine my body still as concrete, I hear a soft breathing that isn't mine.

A lighter twirls in and out of my fingers, knocking against my knuckles. There is fluid inside – and fire. I can smell woodsmoke, like the day I met her, both of us buttoned up in our yellow raincoats.

I put the lighter down and look towards the window.

In that moment, we are both lifting our hands to sunlight streaming through blinds. One of us will see palms glowing with warmth – and one of us will see light filtering through skin that is more and more translucent with each passing day.

The Four Kind Women

Melody Razak

The women are very kind. Their gentleness bewilders me. They smell of almond oil and stewed mutton. They hop on flat feet like crows, whispering from inside their black chadors. They think that because they speak a village dialect I can't understand them, but I can. They're talking about me. Little moosh, they say, so far away from home, her bones so brittle we could chew them, pick our teeth with them. Her marrow would taste so tender in a stew. They lick their lips. Look at her eyes! Have you ever seen such a colour?

They want to eat my eyes.

I think they want to eat my eyes.

I close them at once. I don't want to be seen.

I'm not here and I am here. Consciousness evades me. When I am awake, I feign stupidity. I will not talk. I can't remember my name.

It hurts to move, so I stay still. One of the kind women sits beside me and with great care, as though I am a child, begins to spoon thin soup into my mouth. I purse my lips, refuse. Another kind woman pinches my nose. My mouth opens, the thin soup trickles in and is good. Some of it sticks to my stomach. Some of it they clean with a damp cloth from around my chin. The soup is different here, spicier, darker.

It hurts to eat.

'She's not used to it.'

'She's not had it before.'

'She must eat it. It will nourish her. Fatten her in time for the wedding.'

'Little moosh, so far away from home.'

Wedding?

I don't stink of my own piss and shit any more. Someone has cleaned me, bathed and scented me. There is a whiff of talcum powder on my skin. Rose.

At night I wet the bed. In the morning I leak hot blood on the mattress. The four kind women lift me and change the sheets. They use damp towels to clean in between my legs and when they do this, they do so with sorrow and the fourth woman, the youngest, always cries. They comfort her, bring hot tea and stroke her head.

It's almost as if my wounds are not my wounds alone, but hers too. It annoys me. This sharing of the wound.

We live in one bare room in a big house. The four kind women sleep on rolled-out mattresses on the floor and I have the bed.

The four kind women pray five times a day. I watch them perform their ablutions with half an eye. They wash their hands, their feet, faces and necks, even inside their ears. They mutter and lie prostrate on pink prayer mats, marked by the soles of their feet, and they face the same way.

In the evenings, the four kind women read from the holy book. They take it in turns to sit by my side.

I am not stupid. I know it's not company on offer. It is a keeping-an-eye.

I begin to heal. One day, I can move my arm. The next day I move my leg. On the third day, I sit up in bed. The four kind women are so pleased they coo like warm-throated pigeons and bring me a dish of sweetened cream.

I listen to them talk and learn that I am over the border.

'A pity she is mute.'

'It is appropriate. Anything else would be difficult.'

'It's a blessing.'

Oh. I had not wanted to make it easy for them. I have landed myself in a catch. I will need to find another way of inflicting harm. Do I really want to harm them? Yes. I do.

'It will suit baby brother perfectly, him being so simple himself.'

'She has been sent to us from Allah.'

'She is a gift.'

'A miracle.'

'You will be married soon, dear child,' says the eldest kind woman. 'A modest wedding. Just us and your husband-to-be. He saw you when you were sleeping. He loves you already.'

'Mashallah, little moosh.'

I will do what I am told, and when I am strong enough, when I remember, I will work out how to get home. This, this is not home.

'Today is your wedding day,' says the eldest of the four kind women.

Of course, I know their names by now but I will not

acknowledge them.

They help me off the bed, put me in a tub of warm water and bathe me. They rub me with jasmine-scented soap, wash and oil my hair, dress me in silken undergarments and whilst they dress me they sing in rounds and harmonies that are beautiful to hear. Beauty hurts me. I sob, inconsolable, until I am sick and dry. Ever patient, the four kind women bundle me in towels and wipe my mouth. They talc me as though talcing is the cure for all grief.

They place gold earrings in my lobes.

'Pretty one.'

'Jewel-of-our-hearts.'

'Allah in his greatness has blessed us.'

'You are one of us now.'

No. No, I am not.

They guide me. Help me walk. I have not left the bed in days, weeks, perhaps months? They lead me through a garden and the air is cool on my face. It must be nearly winter. If it's nearly winter here, it will be nearly winter over there.

Imagine a room with two red-bowed high-backed chairs and I must sit on one, and I don't want to sit on one, knowing what it would mean to sit on one, but gentle hands push me gently down and keep me gently in place.

The carpet is all shades of dark blue. It has a gold border of dusky roses and there are peacocks in the centre. I have never seen so many peacocks before, their plumes in fanned coquettish display.

Marzipan-stuffed dates are pushed between my lips.

'A wedding is not a wedding without delectable morsels to sweeten the heart.'

The four kind women take it in turns to kiss my face, and

they are so kind and so full of love when they kiss my face that I almost begin to cry with something like hate, though I don't know yet that this is hate, having never known such revulsion to be possible before.

Two men enter the chamber. The first man is shy. Awkward. His mouth is twisted out of shape. He looks at his feet.

The second man looks straight ahead and when I look at him, prodded as I have been to look at him by the fourth kind woman because one must respect one's elders, I smell him, like a bottle of vinegar pushed to the nose, before I catch his eye.

I remember.

The shock of the flood is caught in my throat. My knees shudder. My stomach heaves like dry rot pickling and all along my spine ice-cold sweat stinks. I vomit. I am like a struck thing. My skin blanched and peeled off, my ligaments, bones and muscles exposed. Marzipan-stuffed dates are all over my dress and the fourth kind woman is quick to clean me up.

The man with the vinegar smell catches my eye for a second and then he looks away. He will never look at me again.

I stare at the dark-blue carpet for ages. I am married to the man with the twisted mouth and simple brain. He sits next to me, blushes crimson. My husband.

After the wedding feast, I am led into a new room.

'This is your marital chamber.'

'Where you will lie with your husband.'

'He blushed when he saw you!'

'You will still sleep with us in the zenana.'

71

'We are always separate from the menfolk. Allah requires it.'

'But for an hour each day, you will lie here and do your duty by your husband.'

'Sisters, does she know?' asks the fourth kind woman.

The other three are silent. The eldest gives the youngest a look and there is something in that look that fills them all with shame.

'Allah. Forgive me. I am stupid to ask such questions.'

They guide me to the bed and lay me on it. They remove my garments and massage my feet. They dab droplets of blood from my thighs and dust them with talc. Rose. They place a brand-new cotton sheet across my naked trembling body.

They look at me in adoration, in envy.

The eldest kind woman uncorks a small vial and feeds me drops of bitter liquid. She has been holding the vial in her hand all this time, hiding it in the clench of her fingers as though it were a secret.

'This will help.'

'It will be over before you know it.'

'It is never enjoyable.'

'But it is a duty.'

'And then there will be a child.'

'A child will bring you joy.'

What is joy? I am growing sleepy. What is joy? I sleep.

I come to with a thick head. The man with the twisted mouth is next to me. My husband. I try not to look at him, but there is an unfamiliar movement and my eyes are drawn involuntarily across. His hand is in his pyjamas and he is frantically touching himself. He heaves a heavy release, leaks a tiny patch of moisture on the cotton crotch, grunts like a baby pig snuffling and then he falls asleep.

Oh!

This, the daily act of my husband frantically touching himself, touching his cock, too simple, too timid to actually look at me, becomes the pattern of our marital bed.

This is joy. It is small joy but I will take what I can get.

I continue to heal. I learn to walk. I go to the toilet by myself. I feed myself.

I learn that the four kind women are the wives, mother and sister of the man with the vinegar smell. There are other women too, servants and cooks who flit around like vagrant spirits and never once catch my eye. They are always cleaning. Sometimes there are guests, women in black chadors, but I don't see them. I hear them. I smell the saffron tea. I am kept in the bedroom and then I know for certain that I am not free. I am a secret and the door is always locked.

My nipples and belly swell. The four kind women examine me with shrewd sideways glances.

One day, I am allowed into the garden. The garden is full and rich with shrubs and flowers in bud, desperate to bloom. I dig my hands into the earth and like a starved seedling turn my face to the winter sun.

The four kind women watch me with pleasure.

'We should let her sit outside for an hour a day.'

'I have not seen her so happy.'

'She has lost so much.'

'Sun spots will stipple her complexion,' says the fourth kind woman with an almost-there-but-not-quite sly upturn of the mouth.

73

There is a boy who tends the trees. He lives in a small hut at the bottom of the garden. I see him from the corner of my eye, looking at me, trying not to look at me, trying not to be seen looking at me as I sit on the ground beneath the guava tree.

The four kind women instruct the boy to stay in his hut between 3 and 5 p.m. so that I can sit outside and put my fingers in the soil. He is not to approach me. It would be a sin. Punishable by flogging. They are stern about this and of course he agrees. He has no wish to be flogged.

They dress me head to toe in a billowing chador several sizes too big. My shroud. They watch me carefully at first, as I sit beneath the guava tree, but it is boring watching me. They grow sleepy and yawn, go inside for an afternoon nap. I sit there for two hours and talk to the tree.

I tell the tree my plan. The leaves rustle and try to dissuade me.

The four kind women have not always lived in this room. They all agree that the rose water here is not as rose-scented as the rose water over there. There is no kebab seller here on Friday nights, behind the Jumma Masjid, grilling and chilli-pepper adding, rolling the meat of the newborn lamb into the pliable naan and twisting it up in newspaper. A roll that to bite into, they all agree, juices on the hem of the hijab, was the closest thing to paradise, as they knew it.

They had not necessarily wanted to cross the border. They were just told that that was what was going to happen. Here, they're not allowed out at all. Not yet. The streets are awash with fresh unrest.

'Do you think we will ever be allowed to go to market?'

74

'Inshallah.'

'Do you think we will ever make friends?'

'Allah will provide.'

'Did you hear the gunshots last night?'

'They say it is worse across the border.'

'What kind of border is it?'

'A line on paper and men with guns.'

'I'm not sure I like it here.'

'It was better over there.'

'Our house was nicer. We had furniture.'

'For shame. This is God's chosen land. When matters settle, we will send for our things. Our home will be ours again.'

'Do you really think she has been sent as a gift?' asks the fourth kind woman, eyeing me up and down.

'Yes. A gift from Allah to reward our faith.'

The fourth kind woman, the second wife of the man with the vinegar smell, likes it best when they cover my face with the veil. A bud of envy unfurls at the back of her eyelids, like a bright-green fern in the monsoon rain. She tries to pretend it's not there, but I smell it. It smells like sour milk.

One day when the air is crisper, the eldest of the four kind women wraps a wool shawl around my neck and whilst doing so feels each of my breasts. My breasts are swollen. I flinch. I don't want her to touch me.

'Daughter! Daughters-in-law! It has happened,' she calls out.

'What?'

'What?'

The fourth kind woman puts a hand on her stomach. 'A

baby,' she says, softly.

In the garden, my legs buckle. I sit on the ground. A new kind of nausea rises to my throat. I put a hand over my mouth and swallow my vomit until I can't swallow any more. I spit into the nearest bush. The bush is dark green. It will flower red hibiscus in the spring.

The boy is in his hut, as instructed to be. Nevertheless, like all people who are told to do one thing but are then, on account of being told, compelled to do the other, the forbidden thing, he stands half in and half out of the door. He watches me vomit.

When I finish and turn around, the footsteps recede. There is a handkerchief on the ground behind me, and a steel cup of water. The handkerchief smells of cheap brown soap, of the buy-by-weight variety. I almost don't want to use it and really how dare he approach me with such stealth when he has so specifically been warned against approaching me at all?

Loneliness wins in the end. I rinse my mouth and wipe the faded cloth across it. The handkerchief is soft on my skin. It might have belonged to his mother, or his sister. I don't suppose he has a wife. I tuck the handkerchief into my sleeve and leave the empty metal cup on the ground.

If I sit beneath the guava tree several days in a row, the boy will know that that is where I'll be. He will watch me and I will like being admired so long as he doesn't come too close. I am not sure by what logic or sense I have worked this out, but somehow I just know.

Every day at three in the afternoon, I sit beneath the tree and wait for the boy to come and ask for his handkerchief. He doesn't.

Fizzy restlessness gets the better of me. One day, I pep

myself up with encouraging words, one eye on the big house to make sure I am not being watched, and walk to his hut. My cheeks burn. The palm-frond door is slightly ajar.

'The guavas are pickling on the tree,' I say. The absurdity almost makes me laugh. This is the first sentence I have spoken in months. 'No one has thought to pick them. They will ferment up there. They will spoil.'

The boy laughs, a warm inviting sound.

I push the palm-frond door open and go in. It is a dark, not unpleasant hut with a narrow bamboo bed nudged to the corner.

'Can you pick some guavas from the tree, and put them beneath it, so I can find them and eat them tomorrow? I'm craving sour fruit.' And then because I am already in the hut so I might as well, I sit on the edge of the bed. He is surprised and then he is not surprised. There is safety in my black shroud.

'This is yours,' I say and give him the handkerchief. 'I washed it. What's your name?'

'Bhaumika,' he says. 'It means from the earth.'

'I can't remember mine,' I say. 'Where are you from?'

'From the South.'

'Why are you here?'

'I came for work.'

'Your skin is very dark. You look a bit dirty.'

He averts his eyes, unnerved. 'I'm outside all day.'

'They will wake up soon. I should go. Don't tell them I can talk, OK? They think I'm mute.'

'Even your husband? Does he think you're mute? I'm not going to tell them. They'll blame me that you're here.'

I flush beneath my shroud. 'My husband is a stunted

77

idiot,' I say. 'I didn't choose him.'

The boy nods sympathetically.

The next day, there are three guavas beneath the tree. I lift them to my nose and inhale the heady perfume.

I go to his hut. The palm-frond door is open. 'I have the guavas,' I call. 'Do you have a knife? I'm not allowed sharp things.'

He comes out. Puts an old jute sack on the ground for me to sit on and on a scratched tin plate he slices the fruit into quarters with a paring knife. He places the tin plate between us.

'Shall we eat from the same plate? At the same time?'

'I only have one plate,' he says.

'How old are you?'

'I'm not sure. I've never known my birthday,' he replies. 'How old are you?'

'I can't remember.'

'Have you forgotten everything?'

'Not everything.'

He brings me water to wash my hands. I dry them on the hem of my shroud.

'You should go. They will wake up soon.'

'Each day I hope they will die in their sleep, but each day I go back and they are still alive.'

He laughs. 'You don't really wish that do you?'

'I do actually. If I could poison their food I would.'

'You don't seem that type of person.'

'Don't you know that everyone is that type of person now? War will do that.'

'For someone who has forgotten so much, you seem to

know a lot about a lot.'

'When I was across the border, I liked to read. My brain is full of useless information. For example, did you know that rats will eat their own tails before they die of starvation?'

'No,' he says. 'I didn't.'

That evening at the allocated hour, in the marital bed, my husband one hand on his cock as is his way, the four kind women with an ear pressed to the door as is theirs, I look at the wall and think of the boy and whether his skin smells as dirty as it looks. I imagine pressing my nose into his skin, so that my breath leaves a moist patch in the crook of his arm, the crook of his arm being specifically that hidden bit inside the elbow.

I sleep. I dream. The boy's dark arms from fingertip to elbow covered in grime that is not the soil of the earth, but the mucus, the blood and guts of a human. Of me. I wake up. I am cold all over.

It is midwinter. The four kind women watch me and whisper amongst themselves.

'Is it normal to sit outside in the cold?'

'Should we stop her?'

'How can we deny her? She has suffered so much.'

'I'll ask the servant girl to keep an eye,' says the fourth kind woman.

A few days later, when a servant girl is sent to keep me company, I am so furious I hit her. I slap her and push her to the ground. Go! She curls into herself and I pummel her small body until she cries out in pain.

I march back up to the house, stand in rigid fury above the

four kind women who are dozing. I clench my fists. I scream.

The noise of my scream comes from some deep unknown place inside me. Deeper than my longing for the boy in his hut, deeper than the food forced through my lips, deeper than my husband with the twisted mouth and back to the night, to the exact time and place when I was dragged off a train and punched in the face by the man with the vinegar smell. I had screamed like this then too.

I was on a train. I had tomato sandwiches in wax paper, a red ribbon in my hair. I was going to see my grandmother. I was raped. I was left for dead. A curious contrition must have got him in the end, because he came back and fetched me. A girl-bride for his simple brother.

The four kind women flap in agitation.

'What has happened?'

'What shall we do?'

'Be careful. The baby.'

'The servants will hear. They will tell the neighbours.'

'The neighbours will tell their friends and relatives.'

'They can't!'

'Shhh. Little moosh. You shall have your heart's desire.'

'We are indulging her,' says the fourth kind woman, the bright-green fern behind her eyelids unfurling into existence.

We are complicit, whispers the eldest and most knowing of the four, but she whispers this only to herself, too ashamed to say it out loud.

I stop screaming. I listen with interest as they panic. I sit on my raised bed and refuse food or water. When they bring the servant girl and question her, she exaggerates so much they don't know who to believe, only that no matter what, there can't be screaming of this sort again.

They whisper, worried. The baby.

They try to push food through my mouth as they did when I was weak, but I give them a look so fierce, they stop. They are afraid of me.

I go to the boy's hut every day now. I sit on the edge of his bed.

In an old saucepan balanced on a metal grille, over a small wood fire, he puts tea and crushed cardamom in boiling milk and because sugar is rationed, he uses local honey, purchased on the black market. He cleans and polishes two condensed-milk cans for us to drink from.

'I heard you scream.'

'I shocked myself.'

'I saw you hit the servant girl.'

'I was angry. They had sent her to spy on me. They don't trust me.'

I drink my tea and smile. The tea in the boy's hut tastes like the tea at home.

The winter air is cold. The boy gives me a hand-stitched blanket and builds a newspaper fire in the middle of the hut. I tell him stories about tigers and djinns and fairy kingdoms. He tells me about the sea.

'When you are in a boat on the water, the wind whistles in your ears and you can taste the salt on your lips.'

'I've never seen the sea.'

The next day he brings me a small fish from the market. I poke it with the tip of my finger and stroke the scales so that they prickle sharply before falling back into place. The fish is iridescent.

Brick Lane Bookshop Short Story Prize Longlist 2019

'I've never seen a real fish before,' I say.

He sharpens a knife against a stone, feels for the vertebrae, slides the blade along the thin frame and deftly cuts the fillet away from the bone. The long thin skeleton is delicate and the cut so clean that there is no gut wound, no bleeding of the organs. I had not thought death could be so clean.

He spears a flake of flesh on his knife and holds it out.

'I can't,' I say, squeamish. 'It's not cooked.'

'Go on. It will taste of the sea.'

I try it. I close my eyes and pretend I am on the seashore.

'You are fearless to come here every day,' he says.

'You would be fearless too. If what happened to me happened to you.'

I tell him about the baby growing in my belly.

'I know,' he says.

'How?'

'Servants talk.'

'What do they say?'

'That you are with child.'

I look at the floor. 'If I tell you a secret, will you still be my friend?'

'Yes.'

'No matter the secret?'

'Yes.'

He spits on his palm and holds it out. I spit on my own and we shake. His hand in my hand.

I tell him my secret and wait to be banished. I don't look up from the floor.

'It happened to each of my five sisters,' he finally says. 'In my village, our landlord took his property as he deemed fit. It was considered an honour that our womenfolk were beautiful enough. It is a strange thing to witness your father beg and plead with another man, when you are just a child. It makes you think that you too will spend your life begging and pleading for things that you should not need to beg and plead to protect. If I had stayed I would have killed the landlord and then I would've been shot. Ma forced me to leave. She was not ready to see me die.'

'Oh,' I say and look up. 'Oh. So you know?'

'I know.'

The boy's eyes are black-coffee-coloured. His skin is like dark wood, like walnuts in their shell. Of course he is beautiful.

He gives me a pencil and a blue airmail envelope with red go-faster stripes along the edge. The envelope unfolds into a sheet of paper.

'You could write a letter,' he says. 'If you remember your address. I'll post it. There is a new post office in town.'

'Write a letter home?'

'Yes. They say at the post office that letters are travelling easily across the border now. Girls who were taken are being rescued. There is a new law. An Abducted Girls Recovery Law.'

'Oh. A saving-face law you mean? By the very men in the white houses who caused the war in the first place?'

I write a letter to my father, but of course I can't remember the address.

The fourth kind woman has started to bathe in orange-blossom water. She arranges choice morsels on a plate and

83

takes them to the chamber of the man with the vinegar smell. In sleep she is restless. She wants a baby. Her own baby. She can't take her eyes off my stomach.

The cashew-sized baby in my belly grows, and I start crying over nothing.

'It was the same with my sisters. First you're sick, then you cry, and then you are full of joy. The more you swell, the happier you feel.'

I shake my head. No. 'There is no joy in this.'

I get bigger. 'Look how big I am,' I say to the boy, crying. Even in despair, I am vain.

'Did you know,' I say one day, 'that he has never once touched me? Not in the way that a husband should touch his wife. I don't think he knows what to do.'

'I did know that.'

'How?'

'Gossiping servants.'

'So, you know then that the baby can't be his?'

'I guessed it.'

One day the baby kicks. I am so startled, I yelp.

'Feel this,' I say and take off my shroud, lower my pyjama bottoms. 'Put your hand on here,' and because he is hesitant, I take his wrist and put his palm on my belly.

He breathes in the wonder of it. The wonder not of the baby's lively foot demanding attention, but the wonder of his own hand, etched with daily graft, placed on the smooth milk of my belly.

'Can I kiss you?' I say and kiss him quickly on the mouth.

He tastes iridescent.

He kisses back. Slowly. Gently probes the inside of my mouth with the tip of his swollen tongue. I want his hand inside me. I want him to reach up and feel the wet warmth of me so I take his fingers and guide them inside.

He gasps. He was not expecting that at all.

The old wounds unravel and unroll to reach my tender heart. I am full of tiny aches. I bleed on his fingers.

His breath is short. I can feel him burning so I move against him. Put my hand on his cock. I whisper in his ear.

'People kill babies all the time,' I say. 'Especially if the baby is a girl.'

He doesn't answer. Doesn't look at me, but I know that he knows it was always going to be this way.

The Weight of Nothing

Toby Wallis

Someone had put a tiny wool hat on Oliver's head but they didn't know who. They had never seen that hat before. Oliver lay in the cot, with the motor that powered the chiller tucked away beneath. Sophie and Will stood side by side, looking down at their son. Linda, the counsellor who was looking after them, stood two steps back. They kept expecting to see little movements. His closed eyes to flicker or his fingers to curl. For him to stir and begin crying.

Sophie felt Will take her hand. He gripped it tight.

'Should we touch him?' Sophie said.

'If you want to,' Linda said.

They had spent some time talking before they went into the room where Oliver was waiting for them. Linda had taken them to a small lounge with three chairs and a low table. There was a jug of water that none of them had touched, a coastal landscape on the wall. Sophie looked at the clock and tried to think what she would normally be doing at 10.44 on a Wednesday morning. She had no idea. Will sat forward in his chair, concentrating hard on everything Linda said. She explained how the cot would keep him cold, how long they would be able to spend with him, what they would and would not be able to do. What they would see, how they might feel. The psychological benefits of the process they were about to embark upon. Sophie barely took in any of it. Her mind was turbid, the words were fogged.

The point, Linda had explained, was to create an attachment. And then to let him go.

Sophie took her hand back from Will, leaned over the cot and touched Oliver's cheek with the back of two fingers. She stroked his forehead and the side of his face, touched the tip of his nose. She felt light-headed at the thought that this was who she had carried. This was who she had been talking to when no one was around to hear.

She stepped aside so that Will could get close. He reached into the cold cot and lifted Oliver's hand with one finger, the tiny fist curled around in a lazy grip. Will tried to compose himself but couldn't do it. He cried uncontrollably, and when he tried to speak he couldn't form a word.

They had painted the walls of the nursery a soft green colour. The small back bedroom overlooking the garden had been filled with old junk and packing boxes for years, but they cleared it out and started getting it ready. They cleaned the skirting boards, hung a lampshade for the first time. Once the room was empty and the walls were painted it seemed transformed. They saw a white wooden crib in a shop, but even though they were sure it was exactly the one, they didn't buy it, knowing they should wait.

Sophie had taken pregnancy seriously, reading deeply on the subject and giving up all the things she was advised to avoid. She stopped eating fish because she was worried about listeria and couldn't be sure which were clean and which might have been exposed to industrial pollutants. She gave up unpasteurised milk and deli meat. She gave up alcohol, which she found easy, and coffee, which was more difficult. Will had joined in, giving up everything except the first cup of coffee in the morning, which Sophie insisted he should keep.

In the evenings the three of them sat together on their little two-seater sofa, Sophie drinking herbal tea while Will read out loud. They were sceptical about the efficacy of reading to an unborn child, but they liked doing it anyway. Sophie had enjoyed the simplicity of it, her ascetic family with their low demands.

Linda returned them to the lounge, got some fresh water and left them to sit by themselves. Will wiped his red eyes, blew his nose and then exhaled hard. They sat quietly for a while. Sophie looked out of the window at the cloudless sky and tried to cry, but nothing came.

'He was so small,' Will said.

She nodded. 'He is.'

'Are you OK?' he said.

She sipped the water. Throughout her pregnancy Will had asked if she was OK constantly, fetching pillows or rubbing her feet. Doing what he could to keep her comfortable. Now when he asked she wasn't sure what the question meant.

'I'm OK,' she said.

'It was harder than I thought it would be,' he said. 'But I'm glad we did it.'

Sophie wondered why she hadn't cried, and she was worried Will was wondering the same thing. When she had stood looking down at Oliver she had felt a rush of blood in her chest, and she wasn't sure if this was love or something else. But for the moments she had stood there, stroking his cool skin, she had felt calm, as if she was standing in the right place.

'Are you sure you're OK?' Will said, but at that moment Linda walked into the room.

'How are you both doing?' she said.

Sophie turned to her.

'I want to spend more time with him,' she said.

Linda nodded. 'Of course.'

For a moment Will looked uncertain. Then he reached out and took her hand.

'I want some time with him alone,' she said to Will. 'If you don't mind.'

Sophie followed Linda down the corridor back to the room. The whole building was quiet. People talked in low voices and their footsteps were hushed on the carpets. She watched her feet as she walked and it seemed as though they were further away than usual. On their way they passed one of the other counsellors coming in the other direction.

'Linda, can I borrow you for a moment?' she said.

Linda shook her head. 'I'm holding a family at the moment.'

The notion of being held made Sophie feel lighter, as if nothing too much was expected of her.

The counsellor nodded. 'Of course,' she said, and carried on her way.

In the room Sophie sat in a chair next to the cot and a nurse lowered Oliver into her arms. He was wrapped in a blanket, keeping the cold in. She held him still, his head resting in the crook of her elbow.

'Is there anything else that you need?' the nurse had said, and Sophie, looking down at Oliver's unmoving face, said that there wasn't.

The nurse closed the door behind her and Sophie sat in silence. When her arm started to ache she ignored it, and even after it had gone numb she tried to hold her son as still as she could.

The next morning Will got up at five and went for a run. This was unusual behaviour. His running shoes had been in the bottom of the wardrobe unused for a long time before he took them out again.

When Sophie woke up his side of the bed was empty but he had smoothed the sheets and arranged his pillows. She expected to find him in the bathroom, or the kitchen, but he wasn't there. She checked the nursery too. The door was closed because Will always made a point of closing it. Inside, the morning light was soft on the pale-green walls and it still smelt of fresh paint. Will wasn't in there either. She walked inside and stood in the centre of the empty room.

'It's not a big room,' she said, 'but it would have done you for a while.' Her words echoed and then were gone.

When she left she pulled the door shut behind her because she couldn't stand the thought of hearing Will close it later. She put a jumper on over her pyjamas, turned up the heating, made herbal tea and sat quietly in the kitchen.

When Will got back he was red-faced and out of breath. His running shoes were damp with dew and stained green and brown. He kissed her lightly, and she could smell the fresh

91

sweat on him .

'Coffee?' he said.

'No thanks.' Sophie held up her herbal tea to show she already had a drink.

He put the kettle on and went to the cupboard for a mug, but there weren't any in there. He took a dirty one out of the dishwasher and cleaned it.

'How was your run?'

'I'm really out of shape, but it was good. I went through the park, down to the lakes.' He turned and leant on the kitchen worktop while he waited for the kettle to boil. 'It's like I can't think while I am running. My brain just closes down for a while.'

Sophie felt it seemed unreasonable, this voluntary closing down of thought. She had struggled to sleep because every so often she would wake in a panic, thinking she had given birth and then absent-mindedly gone home, leaving her child behind. For a few long minutes she would lie in bed feeling hollow and panicked as it came back to her. It didn't seem right that Will could switch off from all that.

'Are you sure you wouldn't rather have a coffee?' he said as he poured his.

And even though she did want a coffee she said no because she wasn't quite ready to go back to it yet.

The hospice staff helped them to make memories. Linda had explained the principle to them. Something tangible so that later they would know he had been here.

They took photographs of Oliver out in the clinic's private garden. The morning sun was bright and low in the sky but the air was crisp. Daffodils were starting to bloom.

Linda kept a close eye on the time, making sure Oliver was not out for too long. They took pictures of themselves holding him wrapped in a crocheted blanket that had belonged to a grandparent. Sophie, not wanting to look at the camera, looked down at Oliver's face and tried to pretend no one was taking pictures. Will didn't know what to do with himself. He held Oliver and looked straight at the camera. In half of the photos he looked solemn. In the other half, unsure.

They were invited to join in with making a mould of Oliver's feet and taking handprints, but neither felt as though they could do it. Linda told them this was fine.

'I'm going to go home,' Will said. 'There are things I need to do, and you can spend time with him alone again.'

'You don't have to,' Sophie said.

'This morning was a lot for me,' Will said.

'I know.'

'Did you want time alone with him again?' Will said.

Sophie nodded.

Will held her close and she could feel the vibrations in his chest, as though he was holding in more tears.

Linda offered for Sophie to wait in the lounge while they took the mould of Oliver's feet, but she decided to go for a walk along the towpath instead.

She bought lunch from a sandwich shop and sat on a bench by the river. On the other side, two people stood on the bank with a pole, trying to hook a shopping trolley out of the water. They were struggling to reach it, leaning over the reeds. Sophie wasn't hungry but picked at the sandwich anyway.

There wasn't much evidence that Oliver had ever been

93

here. A few ultrasound images. Some keepsakes. A book that Sophie's mother had read to her when she was young, saved and returned, the circle completing. The photographs they had taken would be added to the collection, along with the blanket they held him in. They never received either certificate for him. Oliver was listed on a different register.

She tried to think what they would do with it all now. These things that they would keep for ever but would hardly be able to look at. They would have to buy a box, she thought. A suitable box.

Sophie broke apart the bread of her sandwich and fed it to the ducks, carefully separating the cheese and pickle, not sure if those things were safe for ducks to eat. Once the people on the other side of the river had dragged the shopping trolley out of the water they disappeared back onto their canal boat and left it lying on its side in the grass.

'He's started going running in the mornings,' Sophie said when she got back to the clinic.

Linda sat with one leg crossed over the other, holding a cup of tea in both hands. She nodded.

'He was gone by the time I woke up,' Sophie said. 'I'm glad he does it, if it's what he needs to do.'

Linda raised one hand to her lips as though concentrating hard. She didn't say anything, letting the words settle.

'It's the first time I have been alone for a long time,' Sophie said. 'Is it wrong that I'm here on my own?'

Linda shook her head. 'There's no set way of doing this.'

'I'm worried he's not doing it right. That he's missing out.'

'Everyone has to find their own way,' Linda said.

Sophie looked out of the window at the clear sky.

'I talk to him sometimes,' she said. 'As if he is still there.'

'You're talking about Oliver?'

Sophie nodded.

'Did you talk to him a lot while you carried him?'

'When I was alone.'

'Have you tried talking to him here?' Linda said.

Sophie had wanted to, but she hadn't been able to find the words. When he was in her arms it was as though her voice retreated inside her. When she opened her mouth to speak there was nothing there to come out.

'I don't know how,' she said.

Sophie sat next to the cot with Oliver lying in it. Linda had asked if she wanted to hold him again, but this time she wanted to sit nearby. She could spend more time with him when he stayed in the cot. Sophie could see the curve of his body under the pastel-coloured blanket, only a slip of his face visible. The afternoon light came through the cracks in the blinds. She imagined he was sleeping. That he might wake up at any moment.

She composed little sentences in her mind, tried to hear how they would sound, then discarded them. She slumped down in the chair and rested her head on one hand. The chiller beneath the cot hummed gently, and behind that she could hear traffic in the distance.

'I wanted –' she said, but her voice seemed too loud, crashing into the room. She didn't finish the sentence.

The imprint of Oliver's feet sat on the kitchen table and neither of them knew what to do with it.

'How was it this afternoon?' Will said. 'Was it useful?'

Sophie thought for a moment, letting the question rest, the way Linda would. She wasn't sure if it had been useful. The idea that it should have utility bothered her.

'It was good,' she said.

By the time Sophie had got home, Will had opened all the windows, taken out the rubbish, put the washing machine on. The house smelt fresh, as though the cool air was hollowing it out. They looked at the relief of his toes, the folds of his skin. She wanted to touch it, to feel how cool and smooth it was on her fingertips, but when they gave it to her they said it would take a couple of days to fully cure. Will stood up and started preparing dinner, chopping fresh vegetables, which made Sophie realise he had been to the supermarket too.

Sophie was offended by his pragmatism. The way that, in the middle of everything, he was remembering to pay the bills, buy the shopping, clean the bathroom. Things ought to be falling apart. There ought to be a collapse. But he maintained everything so that when their son was gone the remainder of their world would be intact. It didn't feel right.

'Are you coming tomorrow?' she said.

Will leaned over the chopping board, slicing an onion thinly. There were shadows under his cheekbones. His head seemed a slightly different shape. He had lost weight but, until now, she hadn't noticed.

'I don't know,' he said.

He dropped the onions into a hot pan. They sizzled and he wiped his eyes.

'We're supposed to be making memories.'

Sophie didn't like the sound of what she had said. They weren't her words. She had taken them from Linda, from the nurses at the clinic, from the pamphlet they had been given to read.

'I think you should come,' she said.

'I wanted to watch him graduate,' Will said. 'That was the memory I wanted to make.'

He turned the heat down on the onions and stirred them with a wooden spoon for longer than was necessary.

Sophie woke up at three, certain she had left Oliver lying in the grass by the side of the river, and then again at five thirty when Will got up to go running. He was being quiet, but her sleep was so light that even the soft noises of him pouring a glass of water in the kitchen and pulling on his running shoes were enough. She listened for the click of the front door and his footsteps on the gravel path, then got out of bed.

In the kitchen she boiled the kettle, opened the cupboard to get a camomile tea bag and saw a jar of coffee. For months those tea bags had been on the worktop, but Will had tidied them away. Now the whole kitchen was clean and neatly arranged. Sophie took the coffee down, unscrewed the lid and held the jar to her nose. When she was younger she had eaten teaspoons of coffee granules on nights when she was trying to stay awake all night with her friends, and then again later while studying for exams. Ever since, she had drunk a lot of coffee. On careless days she drank so much that it made her fidgety and her nerves fizz. The smell of coffee spread through her body, but she felt guilty that she had let this much of it in. Sophie put the coffee back, took a camomile tea bag and dropped it into a mug.

When Will got home he showered quickly and made breakfast. He put two slices of brown bread in the toaster and undercooked them, the way Sophie had always preferred it. The toast was still soft and had hardly changed colour. He spread some margarine over it, cut it diagonally and handed it to her.

'Thanks,' she said.

Will put two slices in the toaster for himself.

'How was your run?'

'It was good,' he said. 'I went through the park and down to the lakes again. I think two miles. Maybe two and a half.'

'That's a lot,' she said.

'I had to walk for some of it,' he said.

The phone started to ring and Will looked at Sophie. She thought for a moment, then shook her head. He picked it up.

'Hello?' he said.

Sophie recognised the sound of her mother, distant on the other side of the phone, like a hollow voice calling out from a seashell.

'She's sleeping at the moment,' Will said.

He had been intercepting phone calls for days. Their families rang a little too frequently, checking in on them, always asking if there was anything they could do. Of course there was nothing, but Sophie wished there had been some small task she could give them so they wouldn't have to feel so useless. But it wasn't that there was nothing she needed, it was that what she needed was nothing. She didn't think she would have been able to explain it properly.

'We're going back to the hospice today,' he said.

There was a pause, then the distant sound of her mother returned.

He held the phone loosely, saying nothing while Sophie's mother talked. He closed his eyes. His toast popped up out of the toaster.

'I'll tell her you called,' he said, cutting her off, 'when she wakes up.'

Will hung up the phone.

'Thanks,' Sophie said.

He sat down at the kitchen table.

'I don't think I can go today,' he said. He was looking at his hands, limp on the table in front of him.

'It's OK,' she said.

He shook his head. 'I'm letting you down.'

Sophie knew she should say something, but she couldn't think of anything. She was thinking about Oliver, trying to imagine him at the hospice. Whenever she went into the little room with the cot he was prepared for her. She wasn't sure how they kept him when she wasn't around. They always asked her to wait while they got him ready.

Sophie reached and put her hands in Will's.

'I'm sorry,' he said.

'It's OK,' she said. 'I know this is hard on you.'

Will nodded. Sophie gripped his hands tight.

'But I'm not finished yet,' she said.

He looked up at her. His eyes were soft and faraway.

'I'll drive you,' he said.

'That's OK,' she said. 'I want to walk.'

Oliver was changing. Sophie could see it in the quality of his skin, the curl of his lip. She held him lightly and sat back in the chair. The way she held him now was more practised and her arm didn't go numb so quickly.

Sophie had taken a longer route to the clinic, walking along the towpath. The weather was brightening so she just wore a cardigan in place of her coat. The shopping trolley was still on its side on the bank of the river. She walked slowly with her hands in her pockets, runners and cyclists passing her by. She had left her bag at home and liked how unencumbered she felt, a little lighter and a little freer than normal, but out of habit she had kept reaching to adjust a shoulder strap that wasn't there.

The weight of Oliver lying in her arms was barely anything, but she liked the feel of it. The nurse had been gentle as she handled him, and just as gentle with the door when she showed herself out, leaving Sophie alone. She looked down at his face. He had always seemed peaceful to her, the curve of his closed eyes, the creases in his skin. But he was sinking deeper, and she studied his face, trying to hold on to it.

From outside in the corridor Sophie heard footsteps approaching and receding as they passed by the door, and once they were gone the silence felt fragile and thin, as if she had come up from underwater.

'I wanted to show you things,' she said. Her voice was soft and low, barely audible.

Sophie exposed Oliver's hand from under the blanket, touched his fingers and spent a while looking down at them, hers next to his.

'I wanted to show you the ducks,' she said. 'I don't know what else. All of it. I wanted to show you all of it.'

Sophie held him a little closer and took slow breaths of the cold air.

Oliver was still, and she was still. It was everything else that turned and moved.

Open House

Emily Bullock

Standing on the corner of Roman Road, Bethnal Green station behind, Freddie Ierubino recalls his childhood rides on the Underground: scuffed pumps, digging his canvas-covered toes into the ridged boards of the Tube floor; writing his name in the weft of the seat covers but only when his mum wasn't watching. Always the burn of cod liver in his mouth which his mum dosed him with. Its oily taste never quite dislodged by the thick spoonfuls of malt that followed.

The open house is today. He saw the Rightmove listing on the library computer (he was supposed to be searching for one-bedders in Bexleyheath, a warden-controlled future, not searching for the past) but that wasn't why he'd left home. He planned to go to the British Museum, to see the new exhibition on Sicily. He'd climbed the station's worn concrete steps, reached the street before he realised where he was. His feet responding to that familiar pattern of his youth even as his knees pulsed with arthritis. This wasn't Bloomsbury; he'd stepped into a museum of memories instead.

Now he is here, there doesn't seem any harm in taking a

stroll. He's retired after all, his time is his own. He hasn't been back to Whitechapel since his father's funeral, over twenty years ago. Like the new Tube disaster monument, white and angled, don't some things deserve to be remembered? He'll just take a butcher's down Roman Road, go to the British Museum after, and still be back in time for tea.

The concrete and brick around him throb with the unexpected heat of autumn; the sort of day that doesn't know itself. Trees in Bethnal Green Gardens have been fooled into bringing out buds, daffodils peek from the mud, even though it's much too late in the year. London's sky is an apricot haze of tumbled clouds. It reminds Freddie of those walks from the bus stop after a day on the building sites. Summer seemed to last forever back then. Arms swinging, money in his pocket, walking tall like a man, even though he wasn't much more than a boy. His dad always kept a step behind; his heavy gaze weighing Freddie down.

He was fourteen when he first started work, or rather, he was that age when his dad caught him skiving at the back of the flats and marched him down to the building site. Freddie thought he'd take a beating for it, but his dad only put him to work on the lathe, shared his sandwich, bought him a mug of treacly tea off the trolley. It was the first time he heard his dad speaking any English and Freddie was ashamed for him.

When they got home Freddie expected his dad to kick the chair out from under him, which was what he did when really raging. But his dad only bashed more brown sauce onto his mash, dosed the sausages with salt. Freddie expected his mum to put the wooden spoon to the back of his legs. But they just sat and ate with only the ticking of the wall clock, the old bloke next door coughing up his lungs, to break the silence at the table.

Freddie put down his fork, said, 'I'm done with school.'

His mum reached over, topped up his mug, replied, 'Dad says you can keep going to work with him.'

Freddie wasn't sure how she always knew what his dad said when he only spoke Italian in the house and they only spoke English. His mum always acted the interpreter.

A woman in a hijab holds her son's arm, walking along the street, speaking some language Freddie doesn't understand. When his dad was senile, in the home that wasn't his home, and Freddie dressed him, changed his soiled pads, it had made him think for the first time how his dad must have done the same for him once. Or maybe not: his dad was always at work – Monday through to Saturday lunchtime.

Saturday afternoon his parents would go down the social. The club kept a table for the Italians of the neighbourhood, not to keep them separate but because the men wanted it that way. They laughed and drank, shouted and brawled, and sometimes they sang; no one else knew what the words meant but the tunes, the crooning, could make you cry.

Sundays his dad would sleep long into the afternoon, waking to make dinner – fish, or pasta, sometimes both. The flat suffused with the smell of oregano, basil, tomatoes, which his dad grew on the balcony. The neighbours had long ago given up complaining about the stink. Accordion music crackled on the gramophone, and when there were no words to be heard above the wheezing notes, the clatter of steaming pots, they were happy together.

A cab blares its horn. A swirl of diesel fumes engulfs Freddie. The mother shakes her son's arm, says something to him. The boy straightens his Spiderman T-shirt, answers, 'I know the way.' She sends him to press the button, makes him wait for the green man before crossing. Freddie follows behind.

Double-deckers and lorries drive close enough to lift the edges of his sports jacket. He tastes grit from all those spinning wheels. That's new, on the left, a Buddhist Centre. No one knew about Buddhists all those years ago, or if they did they never spoke of it. Coming back, time and time again, a circle of life only to be finally completed with enlightenment and release. Freddie knows this because him and Connie went to Thailand in 2002. They took a train to Chiang Mai; Connie wanted to go to a monk chat. He laughed at her, said, What did she want with enlightenment? As he waited for her outside, a yellow-robed monk sat beside him on the bench, rubbing his cracked heels. The monk smiled, said, 'We're always on the path.' Freddie nodded but had no idea what he meant.

His feet lead him on, they have control and he is the automaton. Following the straight thrust of Roman Road. And there it is – still standing – Ebenezer House. Freddie stares at the red façade, the yellow accent bricks above the windows, which, as a child, made him think the block was smiling. The small green courtyard is well-tended but iron railings cut if off from the pavement. The kids in the flats used to run down the stairs and straight across the muddy square. Now they'd have to deal with a safety gate first. Freddie runs his hand along the arrow points. Such railings would have been stripped and sold for scrap in his day. But it isn't 'his day' any more.

A group of youngsters hang around the doorway. Probably about to cause trouble, planning it if not actually doing it. Kids get guns and shoot up places these days, or stick blades in each other. But Freddie knows how rage can burn. On his last day at West Street School, he'd wished he had a weapon.

Freddie had held out his hand for the cane but McElroy pushed him over the bench, beat his backside like he was a snot-nosed junior. Every time McElroy lifted his arm to strike with the cane, he brought his hand down on the desk too. Freddie saw the long ink stain marking the brown sleeve of the geography teacher's jacket, looking like an oxbow river. Freddie had only meant to do it once, dip his pen in the ink and flick, but everyone was sniggering, and Freddie wanted to get a proper laugh. He had dipped the pen again, stretched out his arm, flicked, and as the ink flew through the air, McElroy half turned, chalk in hand; the ink hit his lips and chin, dribbled down his sleeve.

Freddie wanted to pay McElroy out. The memory of that humiliation lived with him, but that was the point: 'lived' – he would never have finished the geography teacher off.

A man with a clipboard passes Freddie, heading towards the crowd. He's probably going to shift them, or take their names. But on moving closer, although they seemed like kids to Freddie, he realises that they aren't. Some could be nudging thirty. It's hard to tell these days, with the fashion for narrow trousers making them all gangly as newborn foals. These millennials – he's heard them called that on LBC radio – they'd probably laugh to think a father and son couldn't speak the same language; his dad shouting and waving his hands, Freddie answering in English and always trying to speak for his dad on the building sites, anywhere outside the flat. They got by, but never really made themselves understood. He would learn more from that exhibition of Sicily at the museum than he'd ever learned from his dad.

The man with the clipboard does take names, hands out flyers, marshalling everyone into a queue. He lifts the red board above his head, signalling for attention. 'We'll be starting in five minutes. If you haven't given your details, please sign up.' He has a beard, cut low and sharp on his cheeks. He marches up and down the line in his shiny suit like a boy playing at soldiers.

A couple arrive, edging alongside Freddie.

'Here for the open house?' the young man asks.

Freddie looks at the metal-plated door and the row of buzzers for Ebenezer House. He nods. Freddie isn't a man to believe in fate but coincidences have their own rhythm. He steps into the line. The young man tuts, mutters something to the woman with him. She replies with a hot and flustered, 'How was I supposed to know there'd be so many?'

The estate agent reaches Freddie, grips a pen. He isn't quick enough to think up a lie, and gives his name: 'Ierubino, Freddie.'

Saying it out loud makes him flinch, expecting someone to repeat it back to him and say, 'What an age it's been.' No one does, of course. It's been too long. The only echo he hears (and it's just inside his head) is his mum's voice, slapping against bricks, bouncing about the courtyard like a pumped-up football: 'Freddie Ierubino, get in for your tea.'

There must be about twenty in the queue, including the young couple behind him. They all look like they've come from a day at the park: running shoes, backpacks. There's even a girl with a wide-brimmed straw hat like the one Connie took to keep the sun out of her eyes in Thailand. When Freddie was growing up in the third-floor flat, looking out on black tarmac and yellow streetlamps, he never imagined he'd one day take a guided tour of golden-domed temples in Bangkok, or crest waves in a dragon-painted boat along the shores of Phuket. And when he left the house this morning he never thought he'd end up at these flats. Funny how things turn out.

The estate agent punches numbers into the keypad, leans back, levering the heavy door. Freddie follows the people inside. It will make a good story to tell Connie. When he gets home, after putting the kettle on, cracking open the biscuit barrel, picking out a rich tea, he will say to her, 'You'll never guess where I went today.' She might say, 'Oh, Freddie. What you gone and done now?' Only she won't, of course. She's been gone these past five months.

The girl in the hat holding hands with the girl who's dressed like a boy, in oversize shirt and black boots, three places up in the queue, she has a look of Connie. He supposes them to be lesbians. He's long thought women must be a separate species and the idea of them living, breeding, succeeding together gives him a sense of tingling excitement that his sort might just die out one day. The last of the line; he wouldn't mind that on his gravestone. But anything he wants engraved he'll have to leave in writing with Pew the solicitor; him and Connie never had any children. Nieces and nephews, godchildren, had all dropped off the Christmas-card list over the years. But plenty of other people think they get a say in his future. The doctors said he should carry an alarm in case of falls, the lady from the council arranged meals-on-wheels, the neighbour on the left talked of all the space he had in the house and wouldn't he be better in a nice small flat?

On the first landing, from behind cracked glass, a noticeboard advertises a drop-in centre, a diabetes surgery and a housing meeting to be held next week. Freddie's got his Freedom Pass, his British Museum Member's pass, he doesn't need anything else. He's going to sell up the house, his and Connie's place, and buy himself a small flat closer to the shops – he supposes the busybodies have a point. He has a whole list of things to keep him occupied. He certainly won't be joining any residents committee.

A committee should get these hallways redecorated. The floor is painted with a rubbery grey substance that will probably take thousands of years to rot away, but some yob has tried to speed things up, burned a hole in the middle of it. Freddie steps around the black bubbles, fossilised mid burst.

On the narrow turn between the landings, Freddie realises his coming back here is a mistake. What was he thinking, digging around in the past? It's all over and done with.

For once Freddie knows he should do what he planned to do – go to the British Museum, inspect history from behind polished glass.

He tries to turn and go back down the stairs, but the young couple behind him are too busy to notice. Heads held close, peering at a phone like it is a mirror. He'll have to push between them to get downstairs, and what if the door needs an exit code? What if he's stuck until someone comes by?

There's not enough air down there. No choice but to keep going higher. Past the second floor. They stop at the third. His old floor. All the doors are painted red. Were they always that colour? His hand must have pressed against the paint, pushed his way in, so many times, but he can't recall – blue, maybe.

The estate agent has trouble holding them back; the queue spills into the flat. Freddie feels a jolt of anticipation, peeking through the doorway. He steps inside. The young couple bang into him but he doesn't move. They mutter something – apology or insult, Freddie isn't sure which. He steadies himself against the wall. He might as well be stood in some flat in some other city, some other country. Nothing is as it was.

An antique coat stand is rooted in the narrow hall. Floorboards brightly varnished as if they're something to be proud of. His mum saved for over a year to get harlequin lino laid. Words are framed on the walls, enough to make his vision blur: *Love*; *Home Sweet Home*; something foreign about a pipe.

Freddie shakes his head. He is an old fool, but part of him expected his mum's checked housecoat to flash by the kitchen door, the racing results to trot out from the front-room radio, the sweet muskiness of fried liver and onions to greet him.

The estate agent pops in and out of rooms, wafting a smell of aftershave and mints; offering up measurements and dimensions as if giving benedictions. Freddie loosens his top button. There are too many people. They make polite elbow room like visitors at a stately home.

The girlfriends – or maybe they're married, that's allowed these days – loiter in the hall, checking each room from the threshold without entering. The one with the hat fans herself with the wide brim. Connie always liked young people, watching them with the same joy she had when *You've Been Framed* came on (although she never laughed when it seemed the man falling off the skis or the woman toppling off the boat might have actually hurt themselves). Connie collected sunglasses and jewellery like a magpie; if she saw it in a magazine she wanted it. Nothing expensive, mind, just brightly coloured enough to make her ask, 'Does it make me look twenty years younger?' Freddie wishes now, with all his heart, he'd said 'Yes' just once.

He feels an attachment to those girls, not because the pretty one has the same hazel eyes, the same square jaw as Connie. No, it's something else. He bets they never do anything without meaning to; they look the type to plan things and think that planning makes it bound to happen. He won't be the one to tell them otherwise.

He smiles at the boyish girl and she gives him a nod that says, 'I see you'. No one has seen Freddie for some time. There's no one to remember him as anything but old, and maybe it was selfish to hope he'd be the first to go. What with Connie's Grape-Nut, cottage cheese and Ryvita-eating ways, she should have long outlived him.

Now Freddie knows he'll be the last to leave, probably left in a shared room of a council-run facility, where the staff will be nice but young, so young. One day they'll forget he has trouble eating dry food because of his acid reflux, they'll offer him a digestive and he'll take it because he won't remember he shouldn't, and he'll choke right there in his single bed; biscuit crumbs and vomit.

What a self-pitying fool!

Freddie rubs the stubble on his chin. He didn't shave this morning, everything knocked off the axis that was his usual routine with Connie gone. That was one of Freddie's last memories of this flat: loss striking his dad with such force he never quite stood straight again.

Freddie will never forget how his dad cried when the phone fell out of his hand. It hit the lino in the hallway, cracked it in two. On looking closely now, Freddie sees the crack went down to the floorboards, although they hadn't known that back then.

He places his foot over the split in the wood. The young couple put their palms on the walls as if they can measure the thickness that way. They point out coving, which never used to be there, and coo quietly (so the estate agent won't hear) about 'original features'.

It had been an original sight to see his dad cry. Freddie hadn't been sure what to do. He raised his arm a little to offer some comfort, but the thought of touching his dad after all those years of taking care not to even brush elbows on visits home made his limb too heavy to lift. His dad's sobs became wails; the sort he'd seen on the news from widows in Kuwait, tearing at their black robes, trying to shred the pain from their bodies. Freddie kept his arms at his sides, went into the kitchen, set the kettle on the hob. He stood close to the gas ring, waiting for the whistling steam to smother the sound. He hadn't meant to ignore his dad's tears but there didn't seem to be anything else to be done.

Now Freddie stands in the kitchen doorway again, that memory stops him from entering. A girl with pink hair, and a bolt through her left ear, peers out the window onto the netted balcony. It's all changed, of course. Shiny-white melamine countertops and cupboards. A pot of sugar left on the side. Flies will lay eggs in it. A browning copy of *Metro* sits on top of a recycling box. A calendar by the microwave is two weeks out of date. It's as if the owners have vanished. Freddie has read stories about that in the *Daily Mail*, people walking out on their families, their lives. What would make a person do that?

His mum always said, 'A place for everything and everything in its place.' She was the sort of woman who could often be found with the cupboards open, bottles of brown sauce, malt vinegar, tinned tapioca lined up on newspaper laid out on the kitchen floor as she scrubbed the inside shelves. With a surgeon's precision she'd slide the cloth, soaked with white spirit and lemon juice, into each corner, carefully nipping off smears with a dry duster. She never would have left an old paper on the side, uncovered sugar, or an out-of-date calendar on the wall. Every time they went on their week's holiday to the Isle of Wight, before they left, his mum always set the calendar forward to the date of their return. He used to think it was because she took pride in being organised but maybe there was a touch of superstition about it, too – willing them all into a future together.

Freddie waited all year for those summer trips. The taste of salt on his skin, crackling sand in his socks. Fish and chips on the rocks, throwing batter bits to acrobatic gulls. Waving to the passing ferry, thankful that his turn to leave hadn't yet come.

He feels now that he's the only one left on the shore, waving, and waving, watching everything that was his life sailing across the Solent. But his turn will come.

Freddie heads for the bathroom. He wouldn't mind taking a moment for himself, running his hands under cold water, rubbing his eyes. But the bathroom holds a crowd. Freddie doesn't like the press of shoulders and backs, making him a spectator of the avocado three-piece bathroom set. Someone has tried to bring that 1970s choice of his mum's up to date with palm-print wallpaper and fancy silver light fittings. Someone has tried to mask the flowered tiles with paint, but it flakes and cracks in patches. It looks about as ugly as Freddie could imagine. Someone laughs. He moves away, feeling guilty for being part of that judgement on his mum's taste.

Freddie picks at the chipped blue paint on the wall of his old bedroom. These flats were built to last; that 1950s vision was meant to see them through to the space age. Living on the moon, a phosphorus-bright world high in the sky. It hadn't quite happened that way. Connie became his home. Over the years they grew into each other like ivy burrows into the cracks of a wall. There could be no pulling them apart without the pointing crumbling, the structure failing. But here he is – still standing. How can that be?

Freddie looks around. The girls have gone; the pink-haired one isn't anywhere to be seen. He didn't notice any of them leave. The couple who'd stood behind him in the queue are still there, opening wardrobes as if the contents are for sale too.

The estate agent chews on the end of his pen, staring out the window, probably imagining himself selling a penthouse with a WC1 postcode. He glances up. Freddie sidesteps him into the front room. His mum would have approved of how they have done it out; like a country cottage, all white wood and pink roses. The floor slopes a little before reaching the skirting. Freddie stands in the dip. His mum used to keep her armchair by the window, too, although she always complained about the draught.

It was pneumonia that finally did for her. 'Don't let me die alone,' is what she made them promise at the hospital. He told her they'd be right back.

Freddie had persuaded his dad to go home for a bath and a change. It was embarrassing sitting next to him on the plastic bedside chairs – mustard stains on his jumper, dandruff on his shoulders. They heard the phone ringing before they even put the key in the lock. His dad held the receiver away from his ear so Freddie could hear. 'She's gone,' the voice said. And his father, who often made out he couldn't understand a word of English, knew exactly what the nurse meant. He dropped the phone to the floor.

Freddie hears the front door open, voices in the hallway. Perhaps they will just forget he is here. He is good at silence these days.

The estate agent is talking, seeing off the last of them. He will come for Freddie next.

Clipboard clutched to his chest he fills the threshold, shrugs his shoulders at Freddie. 'It's sealed bids. We've already had offers. But go away, think about it if you like.'

Who is he to say 'go away'? Who is he to say anything?

Freddie thrusts out his hands. 'Go on, clear off!'

His palms slip on the estate agent's shiny suit. Freddie shoves again, driving him towards the front door. Freddie hates him. Hates those polished fingernails, the too heavy silver watch. He is old but the estate agent doesn't see this coming. Freddie has the advantage at last. He gets him out the door. Deadlocks the bolt. Barricades it with his back. Knees bending, sinking to the floor.

Finally the banging had stopped, and the estate agent went from shouting to muttering something into a phone. Freddie certainly wasn't going to open the door to him. He had time to think at least, think about what the day should have been. What it all should have been.

A policewoman arrived with a gentle tapping on the door, a calmness to her voice.

She is still here, calling to him again, 'We need to know you're all right.'

Freddie knows he should tell her, 'There's nothing wrong with me.' And there isn't. But a person's life shouldn't be an open house, for strangers to trample through and pick over, not even knowing what they are looking at, as if someone's removed every label from the British Museum, leaving tourists to guess meaning from those fragments of the past.

From where Freddie sits he sees small planes coming in to land at City airport, mammoth-bellied Boeings rising high after take-off from Heathrow. He should like to go back to Thailand, find that monk, ask him, 'Where is the path?' He turns. The policewoman's lips and nose are visible through the letter flap. Maybe he could whisper it through that thin metal gap, letting all the things he ever wanted to say slip out. He puts his hand over his mouth.

He wants to return: he wants to feel the warmth of his mum's hug as he comes through the door, her housecoat flapping about him; he wants to taste the sweetness of his dad's balcony-grown tomatoes, smell them simmering for hours; he wants to fall asleep in Connie's arms, wake and see her smiling face again. He just can't see the way.

How can he tell the policewoman any of that? He's never had the words, and she is too young to know that life can leave you with only memories, not the touch of skin, the heaviness of a slap, the tingling of a lover's pinch. He places his palm over the crack in the floorboards and knows when his time comes there will be nobody left to speak his name, no one waiting for that call. He holds up his hands – empty. Between his fingers more planes cut across the sky.

Life has a way of flying away, leaving you dispersed, insubstantial as vapour trail, and there isn't any way to gather all those tiny particle pieces together again.

Lowenna's Mother-in-Law

Holly Barratt

At ten in the morning on Easter Sunday, Lowenna's mother-in-law draws her right hand out of the chicken, bringing with it a spill of intestines, blood, and little yellow eggs swelling in their bags like bladderwrack. The string of entrails sticks and stretches, so she yanks, then cuts it with scissors, gathers it all up and dumps it in the sink.

Lowenna feels the hollow of her stomach rise. She runs to the sink and vomits on top of the chicken guts. There's not much to what she brings up, and the acid stings her throat and her eyes. She looks down at the mess of flesh and blood and egg and acid against the dull silver of the sink and feels instantly sick again. Lowenna's mother-in-law puts a bloodied hand on Lowenna's white shoulder, leaving a print.

'I was the same of Dai,' she says. 'Right to the last month, even, if I smelled something bad. No shame in it.'

She picks the vomit-covered guts up from the sink and puts them out of sight in the pedal bin, then squirts some bleach around the sink and runs the tap. The smell of bleach makes Lowenna dizzy, but not sick.

'Wash your hands and rinse your mouth out, Wenna, love. Then help me chop the veg if you're up to it. I've got some salmon for you anyway. Might have some myself. I could do this pescatarian thing, I reckon. Not vegetarian, mind, but I'm with you on fish. Though, have you had any already this week? I have heard you shouldn't do more than two portions – down to the mercury. Although you're probably sick of hearing all that should and shouldn't. I know I was.'

Lowenna knows her mother-in-law is a kind woman and that she's looking forward to her first grandchild. Maybe her only one, with Dai an only child and already forty. Lowenna tries to offset her ingratitude with small favours, and that's why she is in the kitchen, even though raw meat makes her sick and the heat from cooking makes her faint. She sticks her finger on top of the salt cellar, to pick up a few stray grains, and rubs them on her lips for comfort. Then she takes a knife from the block and a randomly selected chopping board. Lowenna's mother-in-law quickly replaces the incorrectly chosen tools with the correct ones without a word. Lowenna begins to slice carrots into discs slowly and unevenly and drops them into the waiting pan. Lowenna's mother-in-law looks over from where she is arranging the hollowed-out chicken on a baking tray and doesn't say a thing about the slices being too thick or too thin to cook properly.

Lowenna is in a white dress and fishnet tights – Dai said once that the outfit made her look like a bride in a Guns N' Roses video and she thought that this might be a good thing so wore it often, although now the tights keep rolling down underneath her belly. Lowenna's mother-in-law wears old jeans, a bright-green T-shirt from the surf shop and an apron that says *Because I'm your MUM* on it. Lowenna's mother-in-law has never asked where Lowenna comes from, or who she was before she met Dai, and, whether it is from politeness or lack of curiosity, Lowenna appreciates this. Lowenna is not as good a storyteller as she should be. Sometimes she wonders whether her mother-in-law might know or suspect her origins, and whether lack of curiosity is really a kind of fear.

Lowenna uses the point of the knife to poke the eyes out of potatoes and her stomach jerks so hard that she almost cuts her finger.

'Is he kicking?' says Lowenna's mother-in-law 'Or she. Still fifty-fifty, aren't we?'

Fifty-fifty is exactly right. This baby may live and thrive and save Lowenna's legacy and her kind. Or it might choke and fail inside her like bulging blood-slick chicken guts, only to be ripped out and thrown away. Lowenna places her hands on what was once, for a short time, her waist, and feels the swell. She feels like rotting fruit. As if her skin will eventually split with desperation and the sweet-plum flesh with its head-swimming smell burst through. In two, three weeks' time, there will be a moment, she's heard, when the baby starts twisting and kicking and knocking from the inside, wanting to get out. There's no way of knowing exactly when: in the middle of the night, in bed next to Dai; or lying peacefully on the sofa with his ear soft on her belly saying it reminds him of putting his ear to a seashell when he was young; or in the kitchen with her mother-in-law, whilst chopping vegetables badly and with a fish option thoughtfully half prepared for a dinner she will never eat.

Lowenna has been told she will know. And then she must run. Or run the best she can. Lowenna must leave Dai, and her mother-in-law and the thoughtful pescatarian dinners. She will take off her dress as she runs, and her fishnet tights, and her bra and knickers, the wet grass flicking at her ankles as the air grows deliciously salty and damp, starting to whip the sickness out of her, as all the time the mystery inside her knocks and kicks and scratches. She will go to the cliff edge by Gurnard's Head. And she will stand there for a moment, trying not to look back in the direction of her mother-in-law's cottage, which she persuaded Dai would be a better place for a birth than Bristol. Instead she will look down into the white-lace waves with love and hope. And she'll jump.

She will swim out for a mile then dive deep, deep down, until she catches the song of her kind, the rhythm of their weakened pulses vibrating through the water, calling her to what is left of home. She'll dive faster and faster, away from her mother-in-law and towards her own mother. The new great hope for her family, who haven't seen a new child in a decade. The new great hope for her people, for whom live births are becoming rarer and rarer and where interspecies breeding fights with incest as a means for survival.

She will feel the answer to their questions happen inside her before she even arrives. Every hope is that as her skin cools and the last of her landsickness drains away, she'll feel the baby streamline in her belly, a tiny diver inside her, swimming together towards their home. The joy will pull them forward faster and faster and when they arrive her mother and her sisters will greet her, ready for the delivery, with faces the same as Lowenna's mother-in-law when she learned of the pregnancy, and Lowenna will be a queen for the rest of her life and never think of the cottage again.

Or she will feel a twisting inside her, a kicking, a desperate bobbing upwards, bouncing against the underwater prison of Lowenna's body. Lowenna will continue downwards towards her home as the baby is dragged unwillingly with her. She will feel the desperate pounding and pushing and grasping and begging. And then it will stop. She will continue homeward because that is the only place left to go now. And her family's expectant faces will change through the same disappointment as she imagines on her mother-in-law. And her sisters, silent and unsmiling, will deliver a human baby, and release it, to float up to the surface, be taken by currents to some beach, where it will be found amongst the rubble of bottles and tyres and Lego bricks, given a name by a policeman, and a quiet land burial. And Lowenna's sisters will feed her cold raw fish and tell her that it's not her fault and that she can try again when she feels strong enough.

And either way Lowenna will never return to the cottage where she chopped carrots unevenly whilst dressed as a bride in a music video. And either way Lowenna's mother-in-law will have no grandchild.

One for Sorrow or, In the Garden of Wasted Things

T. Schroeder

When I arrive at the cottage, he tells me not to worry if I find dead magpies on the mat. They have started flying into the glass door, he says. Perhaps it's their own reflections they are attacking. He hands me the key, a basket of firewood for the wood burner, and a freshly baked loaf of soda bread, then waves as he turns down the path, wading deftly through the floodwater in his wellies, slipping through the arch of rowan trees lining the path to the cottage, and out into the wilderness beyond. He leaves ripples in his wake.

I heave my traveller's backpack onto the bed. It is covered with a crocheted blanket in a sunny lemon yellow. The owners have left me a complimentary jar of honey and some sweet peas in a small glass vase. The sweet peas and the honey glow in the light of the bedside lamp. The rest of the décor is creamy emulsion, mismatched crockery, silvery pots. Several blankets thrown artfully over a faded powder-blue sofa. I write 'I am sunlight' on a Post-it note and press it onto the jar of honey. I write another, 'Call Ma', and attach it to the wall next to the sofa. Then I write out the Chinese letters for my name on a third Post-it and slip this under my pillow.

All night, the rain washes through the hills and I startle at every thump and creak. In the city, I think with a kind of sleep-drugged slowness, there isn't enough room for all this noise. The buildings, the cars – the mess of it – they catch the rain, trip it up, muffle it. I realise with something vaguely resembling horror that I am not sure I have ever *heard* trees before.

I flick the lamp on, then off. I am restless. I gulp down a glass of tap water, dip my finger in the honey jar – such sweetness! – fiddle with the small radio on the windowsill. I crack open a window even though it is really coming down outside, just to breathe in the air which is glassy, earthy. The night is velvety black, and I wave my arms out of the window till they are slick with rainwater.

When I eventually fall asleep, it is into a tangle of dreams about giant birds, enormous magpies with tender white breasts, the inky purple-green of their tail feathers smashing against the walls of the house, leaving a film of iridescence on everything. I hear a woman's voice praying in Mandarin. Dozens of glass eyes sparkle in the darkness.

In the morning there are no dead magpies on the mat, just a clump of leaves. I bend down to inspect them, but have no idea what they are. I know what oak leaves look like, their wonky puzzle-piece shapes a memory from childhood. And horse chestnut leaves, which my brothers would shred to make them look like fish bones. I take a photo and send it to my mother's email address with the subject header, 'Leaves'.

I write again some moments later. 'Did you get my email? I miss you.'

When I first arrived it was getting dark, so I hadn't registered my new surroundings. Now in the watery sunlight I can see the vast stretch of fields and the dip and curve of the hills beyond the paddocks of the smallholding where I have come to Get Away. Tiny birds are making tracks like loops of ribbon. A kite hovers in the distance over a thicket of trees, feathers splayed like fingers.

At home, it had felt like a hive had grown inside my head. The noise was so dreadful I thought my skull would cave in. It wasn't till I said it out loud, at my desk at work, that I realised it to be true. 'I need to get away.' No one even looked up. I found the cottage website using my work PC: *Small eco-friendly cottage, no third-party bookings, the perfect hideaway.* I booked. I left a letter of notice for my boss, Toby, on his desk – Toby, with his face like a loaf of bad white bread, his too-small mouth mashed into it, his waxy dandruffed hair.

Six years. Six years of early-morning commutes, Tupperware lunch boxes, thousands of emails and too many important-not-important meetings to count. Time is not to be wasted, and yet I let it slip through my fingers. Time, my mother said, is invisible until you look down and realise you are knee-deep in yesterdays, and your hands do not look like your hands.

Last week I found five new white hairs sprouting in my parting. Ma had found the first, six months ago, and plucked it out with tweezers. Later, I discovered she'd kept it in a small box on the dresser.

*

I can feel something inside me unwinding outwards as I stand on the porch as if it were some kind of threshold. I curl my fingers around my mug of freeze-dried coffee, breathe in the smell of muck and green and Gold Roast, marvel at the chickens pecking at the ground. One of them shits, a great big white squirt. I retreat into the cottage, switch on the laptop, and click into Word.

Birdsong is stitching the air and I stop and tilt my head to listen.

I receive a message from Ma, reminding me to perform an energy-cleansing ritual. I have a stick of palo santo for this, and waft it through the three small rooms: the living area with its neat kitchenette, the bathroom full of sun from a huge skylight, and the bedroom which smells sweet and dusty. I tell my mother when this is done. I also tell her I am thinking of taking up a new hobby. Perhaps birdwatching, or magic. I could retrain as a teacher, or a social worker, I say. She doesn't reply. I strip naked and lie on the bed till I am covered in goosebumps, then get in the bath. I take the mirror down from the wall.

I write a short observation of myself in the third person, as if I were a character in a book. Reading it back, I bore myself so much I start to get a migraine.

My horoscope app pings. *Mercury is about to turn direct, and with this shift there may be some misunderstandings you will have to deal with.* I puzzle over this while I cook a pack of Super Noodles. Looking out onto the fields, I feel imbued with new energy. I decide to mark in my lunar calendar the night of the next new moon and to do something extraordinary. Maybe an attempt at a Guinness World Record. Or a miracle. Or the best damn beef noodle soup.

I call Ma, but the phone goes to voicemail.

On the third day at the cottage I hear knocking, and come out of the bedroom to find smudges in the top-right corner of the glass in the front door. Magpies. A piece of paper has been slipped under the door. When I unfold it my chest feels like it is filling with cold water. *Coming events cast their shadows before them.* A Chinese proverb. I quickly unlock the door and look outside, but there is no one. No tracks. No sign of disturbance. Below the porch, by the steps under which firewood is kept, a cluster of daffodils have opened their papery buds, splashing bright yellow onto the path. I descend the steps to peek underneath, but there is only firewood and soft hanging webs, a large spider crawling along the shelves, and small gatherings of moss.

I crumple the paper in my hand, stomp loudly up the steps, darting a glance behind me. I lock the door and throw the paper into the basket with the kindling. I try to make myself a cup of tea and realise my hands are shaking.

Later that day I find a songbird, its neck broken but otherwise perfectly intact. I use a tablespoon to shovel it into a grave by the vegetable patch between labels for beetroot and sprouting broccoli, then wash my hands several times. I find postcards in the bedroom. I write one to my mother, and one each to my brothers. 'Thinking of you!'

*

On the fourth day, a spray of shepherd's purse appears, the roots dangling from the stems. I find the toothed leaves disturbing and throw them into the fire, but have to air the place when they sizzle and the stove gives off a smoke that clogs my throat and makes me dizzy. I open all the windows, then sit on the porch and smoke my first cigarette in two years. That night, I hear a low whistling outside, and cannot sleep.

On the fifth day a plant pot sits outside on the mat. When I work up the courage to look inside, I find that it is teeming with earthworms. I throw them into the compost, then slash the heads off all the daffodils around the cottage with a knife and dump those in the compost too.

On the sixth day I find a clutch of broken eggs. They are small, a pale buff with a greenish tinge, and a few darker flecks. Inside they are smooth and white.

For some reason, I am undone by the eggs. I sit for a long time on the porch, a light rain covering me like a veil. I cry, holding the broken shells in my hands.

On the seventh day, I finally make contact with Ma by phone.

My mother is a batshit-crazy Taiwanese woman who used to beat us with her tiny slippers till the backs of our arms were shiny raw. If she was in a bad mood, we'd get a volley of kitchen utensils and a shower of expletives in Mandarin. And if she slung us over her knee with a rice paddle in her hand, we knew we were in real trouble. A small woman, my mother displayed impeccable manners outside of the house, her demeanour as smooth as the burgundy satin jacket that she wore with the same soft-cotton chinos, no matter the season or occasion. But inside the house, she screamed and shouted, was viciously unsympathetic of illness and low grades, or any other barrier to our learning and advancement, constantly angered by how westernised and lazy her offspring had become, reminding us how like our father we were, a man we had never met but knew lived somewhere in Scotland, in a house so full of grief it was like living underwater. Too soft, la, she would say. Like rice in soup. And she would spit on the floor, then make one of us clean it up.

With Mother everything was brightly lit and painful, and embarrassingly strange. We had a Mazu shrine in our tiny kitchen, a nod to the journey her ancestors had made across the Taiwan Strait many years ago, with incense sticks to remember those who did not survive the treacherous journey from the mainland. There was always a pot on the boil in our house, with chicken bones or eggs or mysterious vegetables, and the walls were always clammy from the steam – mould bloomed and was scrubbed back with bleach, then bloomed again. Small jars stuffed with herbs and spices cluttered every free surface, crowding out the pots and pans and plates, the boxes of tin foil and rubber bands and the plastic bags full of plastic bags. The winking mirrors on the walls.

Mother was in a constant battle, with the mould, with the world, and with us, her children. She would remind us of all she had sacrificed, and later, in our shared room, we would share cruelties: left behind poverty in Taiwan for a nice life in England, poor Ma, we would say. Left behind a stupid depressed husband for a good job. Bet he couldn't stand her, bet she made him like that, put him in a coma with all her whining. Left behind her backward family with their muddy feet and dirty goats.

It felt good to be hateful.

We hated that we had to eat lunch out of old margarine tubs, that Mother brought oranges to our friends' houses as gifts and pretended not to notice the other children laughing at her, that she picked her teeth at the dinner table. We hated that we weren't allowed any normal foods in the house even though we begged for pizza instead of bah-tzhang and soup with so much ginger it made us cough. The day my younger brother had his first asthma attack she stripped him of his clothes, his body loose and slippery, and rubbed ointments on his body. It wasn't until his lips turned blue that she let my older brother call an ambulance. He called her a bitch. He could have *died*, he said. You bitch. You crazy old bitch. He was seventeen. For days afterwards the house reeked of incense, but the shouting stopped.

'Daughter, what is in your heart?' This is how she has started every conversation we have had in the last few weeks.

'Ma, something strange is happening.'

'Yes, that does not surprise me. The weather predicted it.'

Outside, the sun is tracking the fields like a blessing from heaven. In the distance the clouds are bruised and swollen.

There is a silence, then a sigh. 'OK tell me. Tell me and I help you this one time.'

I tell her about the gifts, and the magpies that keep flinging their bodies against the glass. She listens, and I imagine her sitting with her hands folded neatly on her lap, her legs dangling slightly above the scrubbed-clean floor of the kitchen, the backs of her slippers slapping against her heels. Sun Yat-sen smiling down on her benevolently from the fridge onto which he has been Blu Tacked for years. She advises me to check the flow of qi through the cottage. Do not allow the energy to flow out of the door. The door should not face a window or another door. If it does, try placing something between them. Open the door daily to allow the energy in. Bring greenery inside to help aid the flow of energy through the house. Check that there is no space above cupboards and if there is, add a living plant. 'There must be a blockage somewhere,' she says, carefully, precisely. 'Something is blocking the energy flow and so you are receiving bad luck and ill omens. Are you sure you do not know what is blocking the energy, daughter?' She sounds sad when she says this, and I change the subject.

'Ma, will you tell me a story?'

'You are too old for stories, Jùnjié.' Ma is the only one to call me by my Chinese name. Almost too quietly to hear, she adds, 'You need to stop calling me, daughter. What is in your heart?'

I ask her to recount the story of the cowherd, Niulang, and the weaver girl, Zhinü, who fell in love after Zhinü ventured down from her life in heaven, where she wove clouds, to explore earth. Upon discovering their love affair, the Goddess, Zhinü's mother, forbade her daughter to return to her earthly life, where she had since had two children and lived modestly among mortals. Devastated, Niulang journeyed to heaven to find his bride, only for the Goddess to scratch a river into the sky to stop them from being together. 'And this is how the Milky Way was created,' Mother says, in the same voice she would use to tell us the story when we were children. Silver River. She pronounces it 'silv-*ah* riv-*ah*' and I smile. My heart feels as if it might burst open like a flower. But their

131

love was so strong, Ma would tell us, as we watched her spin her tale from under our blankets, twitching our feet against her warm body, that once a year, on the seventh night of the seventh moon, all the magpies in the world flock to form a bridge to allow the lovers to reunite. And then my mother, my fierce mother with her snake's tongue and a gut made of steel, would get teary-eyed. I open my eyes. There is a dial tone in my ear. She must have hung up.

'Daughter.'

'Ma. Did you hang up?'

I hear her clucking. 'Hush hush, of course not. You are imagining things. But I must go, you are keeping me. Daughter, we cannot talk like this any more. You have not told me what is in your heart and I am afraid for you.'

'Ma, wait. Please. Stay with me a little longer.' There is silence. 'Ma?'

Her voice is very faint when she speaks again. 'There are no miracles, daughter. There is only what you see. You are not seeing, only looking. You must start with your heart. Try again. Pay attention this time. What do you see?'

Please hang up and try again. Please hang up and try again. Please hang up and try again.

The knocking has started again. Magpies are seen as tricksters, thieves, rascals. I like them that way, ragged and unpredictable, mischievous fate-bringers spinning both sides of a coin. But to Mother they were sacred creatures. She would place offerings on the window ledge for them, though often it was the fat city pigeons that ate her seeds and fruit pulp and leftover sticky rice. One day she managed to catch one by its ratty foot, and screamed at it in Mandarin before letting it go. It careered drunkenly into a wall before flapping its wings and regaining equilibrium. 'FAT BASTARD,' she yelled, in English. We laughed so hard that I peed myself.

As the phone rings on the other end of the line, I close my eyes and picture a flock of magpies gathering between the dial tones, collecting like iron filings around a magnet. Hundreds of magpies falling from all the skies to form a bridge between me and my mother. The bridge stretches between worlds. Today is the seventh night of the seventh moon. It is strange, but suddenly I cannot remember the sound of her voice.

Outside I hear thud after thud. Magpies are falling like a terrible rain.

The phone keeps on ringing, and ringing, and ringing.

The Littoral Zone

Sylvia Warren

Anna knows the way by heart. She has walked it every after-noon, her one hour of solitude from Sara since taking over her care. It takes seven minutes to go down from the house to the edge of the beach, then a further twelve to weave her way across wet-slicked seaweed, past the pools that are only exposed at low tide – those that contain the stranded, the im-mobile, and the unlucky – then finally to the surf. She has twenty minutes before she must turn back, before her guilt occludes the comfort. Seasons tip over each other, sometimes a slow fade and sometimes like missing a step on a staircase, but the walk is always the same.

Summer

It is one of those endless afternoons in midsummer when the heat has dried the grasses into bleached stalks and the sky is heavy and motionless. The local boys are over on a nearby rocky outcrop, teenagers and a handful of younger children, all stripped down to their boxers and shrugging on mantles of confidence. Some suit it, assured and already immortal; the others are still playing dress-up, imitation as a form of self. Anna watches one of the older ones climb up to the top of the rocks, stand for a moment, and jump – he is a wild shout of limbs and gravity and exhilaration until he disappears into the water. It must be different, she thinks, to be able to shatter the silence without feeling the need to ask permission. The boy's head breaks the waves several metres away from where he entered, the splash of his lazy front crawl mixing with the laughter and leaping of the others. The knotted feeling in her chest relaxes, and she turns back.

The house is cool despite the sun outside. Anna drops her keys in a small saucer on the porch table, notices yet another brown envelope on the mat. Sara is her first priority. The house has a peculiar layout. It is a bungalow and the front door leads to a narrow kitchen rather than a hall. It is as though the house had been built backwards, with the logical entrance facing away from the lane and towards the garden. A bungalow is necessary for Sara, now. The sitting room has been converted for her; the bed has railings and a button, so she can raise herself slightly. The bed faces the French windows; a cushioned chair sits in the corner.

'Did you have a nice walk?'

Anna nods. 'Hot. The boys were out, up on the outcrop. Quiet today. Would you like me to open the curtains for you?'

The shape in the bed moves. 'And let me see what I'm missing? No. Lemonade. Mint from the garden. Fetch me my book. You were gone for hours.'

Anna doesn't say that it was fifty-six minutes. She picks mint from the garden, stirs it into lemon juice and sugar, tops it up with fizzy water, finds the book in the bathroom, notices it is overdue, curses. The letter was, of course, about the allowance. Another meeting, in a town over an hour away, so make that four hours for safety, there and back. Find someone to be with Sara, not one of the boys, although a teenager would be cheaper, and nothing should happen . . . but it will probably have to be the woman who lives down the road. A phone call is in order, but if Anna is to pay her minimum wage for the four hours then that will be . . . about £32 which is over a third of her weekly . . . She leans her head against the cool of the counter. There is dust. It has built up and become coated in a thin layer of kitchen grease. The floorboards are sticky towards the edges under her sandals. Everything accumulates, even accidents.

Mary will look after Sara when Anna goes into town, but this isn't a formal arrangement, she says. 'It's not that we are not awfully sorry for what happened to your sister, but, well, things being how they are I can spare this afternoon, but it can't become a habit.' She is sure that Anna understands. Anna does understand. She says goodbye to Sara, catches the bus, changes to the other bus that takes her to the office where they tell her that, as a sibling, she is now entitled to less, although she could cut her sister's disability payments so she could claim a different allowance, but that could leave them both less well off in the long term. Her reality is blurred into statistics and numbers and projected costs and a perfunctory apology for taking up her time on this lovely summer day. Anna leaves the office, catches the first bus, doesn't miss the second bus, walks home, opens the door, drops her keys in the saucer, and Mary is in the kitchen.

'She's been all right, love, spent most of the time asleep.

137

You're a bit late, though, my Jack will be needing his supper, so I'll be popping off . . . Don't worry about the extra half hour, consider it a favour.'

Five minutes down to the beach, stomp-slither over the seaweed, crack a small shellfish underfoot and feel power for a moment before it becomes shame, right down to the peaceful waves lapping against the pebbles. Anna is furious that the sea isn't reflecting her anger. How dare it sit so soft, a playground for children and sea creatures? It should be leaden and spraying salt and foam and scum all over the bay. She takes off her shoes and socks, rolls her trousers up to her calves and walks in. The first lap of salt water closes over her ankles, retreats and pulls the pebbles down with it so Anna's feet sink into the shore, substrate making way for her presence. For the first time this week she allows herself to cry. The sun will not set for another two hours. She lies down, lets the sea form a hollow for the shape of her body, and her heart cools and settles.

Autumn

Sara moves from her bed to the bathroom to her chair. The bathroom is for bathing; she defecates and urinates in a bedpan. 'Anna, come in, don't look!' It has been three years, and Anna still hates the necessary bodily intimacy with her sister. And the shit. She had argued with herself over the cost and the environmental benefits of having a reusable bedpan, or a biodegradable one she could throw in the compost – she wants to be an ethical consumer as far as she can – but putting the bedpan into the sink, heating the water and preparing and disinfecting it made her resent her sister. You choose your battles. Also, in the short term the disposable ones were cheaper.

'Anna?'

'Sara, I'm here. Are you OK?'

'No. My period started. Anna I am so sorry, I am sorry that this happened, I think I have bled over the chair, God, I'm sorry.'

'It is not your fault, these things happen. I'm going to need to move you.'

'Don't touch me.'

'Sara, I do not want to wipe your bloody cunt any more than you want me to clean your uterine lining from between your legs. But this is where we are, so suit yourself. I am not going to do anything you do not want me to do. I've left some tampons on the bedside table. I unwrapped them for you.'

Just in case your fingers couldn't.

'I didn't mean to snap.'

'OK, I've got a bowl of warm water . . . No, oh *Sara* – sorry, sorry. I know you didn't mean to knock it over. It's fine, I'm not cross. I'll wash the chair, it's OK.' Sara has the look on her face that Anna now recognises as pretending she is somewhere else. It makes it easier, probably for both of them. For Anna, there is simplicity in pretending she is doing a practice from the handbook she bought when her role started. Take (a) one washcloth, (b) one bowl of water – dip your little finger in to test for temperature, (c) ask for consent and explain what you are going to do, ((c.i) – not in the manual – deliberately ignore that this is your elder sister), (d) wipe around the labial folds, remove any menstrual blood and clots, (e) talk the patient (elder sister) through inserting the tampon – those with applicators are normally less difficult.

As though it would ever be 'non-invasive' to have someone insert something into your vagina for you, is still Anna's view each month. It would be easier if Sara liked pads, but she says they make her feel sodden and childish. Anna carries her sister to the bed, leaves a couple of ibuprofen on the bedside table with a glass of water ('remember, autonomy in small tasks can be important for sense of self'), strips the chair covers, puts them in the washing machine, boils a kettle, prepares a hot-water bottle, and stands in the kitchen for a moment, holding the rubber flask wrapped in an old towel. Her own uterus gripes, a twisting thick pain – they are sisters living together after all – and she swallows her discomfort and walks back into Sara's room.

'It's almost four.'

'Yeah, I know. Here's a hot-water bottle. Better?'

'A bit . . . You know how it is. Thanks for the pills, they'll kick in soon. Go for your walk, it's getting dark.'

'Are you sure?'

It is a neap tide; the low water rises higher than normal. In the twilight the beach is indistinct, the clouds have muddied the reflections in the rock pools, and the bladderwrack is black and oily underfoot. The air vesicles pop wetly under her feet, hissing out bubbles of salt water. *Littorina* snails cling to the fronds, pale olive and yellow in their shelter. The breeze smells of salt and something else, something marine and ancient, fetched up from the depths by the push and pull of the moon. The sea bleeds into the sky, the line separating the two fuzzy. Anna feels the call at times like this, the sense she has had since she was a child that it should be possible to swim out to the edge of the world and dangle her legs over the horizon. The bay is a shelter, long headlands cradling the shore from the full extent of the ocean's power. She takes the long way home, stopping in to pick up some books from the library.

'How's Sara?'

'OK. Well . . . no, she's OK. Sorry, these are late again.'

'Keeps the place up and running, love. Or up-ish, anyway. Hobbling along.'

'Yeah, it's a disgrace. These four please.'

'Right you are. There's a new one of hers coming out soon, I'll try to get a copy.' The librarian taps a bitten nail on the top book, a thick historical novel by an author Sara likes. Anna nods, thanks her, picks up the books and goes home.

The bedroom is cold. Sara is asleep, her chest rising and falling softly under the duvet. Anna shuts the window quietly, places the books within her sister's reach. She hangs up the clean covers to dry, and slumps down on her own bed. She wakes up later, still fully clothed, and realises that Sara's tampon has not been changed in over nine hours.

Winter

Walking back up from the shops, Anna feels again that coastal villages in winter have a peculiar bleakness of their own. The wind whips a fine spray of salt off the sea that seeps into everything, settles into corners. The entire world is rendered into flat grey – sky, tarmac, weather. Even her hands are colourless, except for the angry red welts where the bags dig into her palms.

Sara calls as Anna opens the door. 'You're back! Thank

God, I've been so bored. I can't work out if I'm more bored by the sight of the curtains or of the bloody view outside, if you can even call it a view. What have we got?'

'Caviar and larks' tongues, as per your instructions.'

'Oodles of champagne, darling?'

Anna unpacks her shopping. Most of it has a yellow label. She has worked out the time on a Thursday afternoon when things are marked down. It enables variety. 'I left the staff to deliver it, couldn't *possibly* carry it on my own. Two mins, your ladyship, I'm just unpacking. Coffee?'

'Oh, poor little Cinderanna, stuck looking after the evil ugly sister. Also, yes, please.'

'Piss off,' Anna says, smiling, puts a mug down by the bed. She drags the chair closer and tucks her legs under herself, holding a pillow to her stomach. They sit quietly for a moment, rain spattering against the glass.

'Sorry I was so long, it's foul out. I bumped into Catrin, by the way. She asked after you.'

'I hope you didn't give her my love. What's she doing now the library's closed?'

'Odds and ends. She's temping in an office, but it's short and fixed term. She said she's looking elsewhere but it's so expensive. Do you think you can manage some toast?'

But Sara is crying. It is not a wail, it is a controlled release of the swallowed grief that she and Anna feel every day. It is the ragged breath that is half anger, half shame, half exhaustion, half sorrow. The halves add up to a greater sum of emotion than can be held within a single heart, which is why it spills out, sometimes in tears or sleeping or silence or violence or absence. It is the result of a continuous act of wave erosion, no matter how slow, until parts of your sense of self crumble into the sea and your whole geography changes. The waves are brown envelopes and meetings and yellow labels and eking out an existence in a world that changes around you, both drowning and desiccating. Anna curls into the bed with her sister and wraps her arms around her.

'I'm sorry.'

'Don't you dare apologise, Saralara. It was an accident. It's not your fault.'

'I'm not saying sorry for that.'

'What do you mean?'

'I mean, fault isn't the point. I can be guilty and not at fault. I've tied you here.'

'I like the sea.'

'If you tell me you would genuinely have chosen to stay here, you are a liar.'

'I'm an accident too, though.'

Sara takes a deep breath and pauses.

'You are not bringing this up again.'

'Well, if that accident hadn't happened you could have had a "proper" carer rather than our parents' little mistake.'

'You think I want someone else?'

'No, that's not what I meant. I meant . . .'

Anna sits up and presses her forefingers on either side of the bridge of her nose. Her vision sparks green and red in the static of her closed eyes. 'I should have been in the accident. I know that. You were the wanted one. It's not fair.'

'Shut up. Shut up, shut up, fuck you. You must feel so fucking virtuous. And yes, you should have been.'

Anna gets up from the bed, eyes red-pricking. 'I'm going out. I'll be back in an hour or so. I know you don't mean that. Do you need anything before I go?'

Sara does not reply. The silence is a dismissal. Anna runs, slipping and sliding over the rocks until she collapses at the uprush, digging her hands into the pebbles and hurling the shore into the breakers. The sea accepts her tears as she tries to return the coast to the water.

She strips. Her clothes lie crumpled on the rocks; she briefly considers what would happen if they were taken. Shivering white in the November dusk she runs in with a scream, no time to stop or ask. The cold punches the air out of her lungs, halts the sound in her throat. She dives under the surface, pushing against the flow that rolls around her. Underwater, she undulates, seal-like and slippery, losing sensation; her limbs freeze and prick with the cold. She front-crawls back to the shore, ink-black splashes and milky annotations trailing in her wake. The sea has washed away her guilt and anger and sorrow to leave only the burning, ferocious love. It is time to go home.

Spring

Anna opens the French windows. She pulls Sara's chair outside, with difficulty. She is a little small to manoeuvre such a solid piece of furniture quietly. The earliest daffodils are flowering at the end of the garden; the sea glitters in the background. She places two wine glasses on the table and fills them, arranges some pineapple chunks on a saucer with a spoon. She puts a bowl over the fruit in case of insects.

She walks Sara to the bathroom, turns on the shower, checks the temperature, then gently guides her in, opening the shower gel.

'What's this?'

'It was on offer, sorry.'

'It smells good. Did you read the bottle? "With a gentle yawn, she stretched and captured her dream . . . It was still warm." Who writes this shit?'

'Someone who can afford to buy non-discount soap. Do you think you can do yourself today?'

'I think so, yes.'

Anna passes her the flannel and sits on the loo seat parallel to the shower. This is when she feels at her most sisterly; they could be getting ready to go on a night out. She has read that sisters do that – they borrow each other's clothes and paint their nails and talk about people they fancy. She was too young to do that with Sara, and when she was old enough they couldn't. The sounds of the water stop. The mirror is fogged.

'I'm done, can you get me out?'

Anna wraps a towel around her sister, rubs her all over, musses her hair. Her body is weak and thin, bones protruding but no muscle, soft like the inside of a slipper limpet.

'Sorry, let me pop you on the loo for a second. Good hold of the handle?'

Sara nods, but Anna runs from the bathroom nevertheless. A nice dress. Thank God for the style of tea dresses recently – straight on over the head, and yet not shouting 'I need an elasticated waistband and no zips or buttons.' A sense of dignity in a cheap dress from a high-street store that ameliorates the stares because it looks contemporary. She had saved up for it. Eight pounds. Adults shouldn't have to save up for eight pounds.

'Aren't the bees lazy?'

'Ms Sara, you are tipsy! You've only had a glass.'

'No, but like, look at them. Buzzing about. Bzz bzz bzzz. Big furry bottoms all covered in dust. And don't call me Ms, you're not my maid.'

Anna is silent. Sara's voice is small.

'Will you take me down there?'

No, you will ruin it, no, this is my beach, this is mine, the one place where I can be alone and not a reflection and shadow of you. No, I cannot think that, I am useless, I am selfish, no.

'Yes, but it won't be comfortable.'

She drags the empty chair over the rocks, tripping and pitching and catching her fingers in the arms and the feet to bring her sister towards the sea. She returns to the house, carries Sara down on her back, fingers interlocked under her sister's bony legs.

'Couldn't you have got one of the boys to do it?'

'Tart.'

'If you prick me, do I not cum?'

'I'm not even going to respond to that.' She can feel Sara's smile on the nape of her neck.

The wind whips across the sea, rhythmic and alive. Wavelets break over each other, swell into each other, meet and diverge, all on their inexorable way to the shore. Sea pink is just coming into bloom. The air is soft and clean. A seagull cries and circles, trembling against the sky with a shaky elegance. Sara's eyes close against the hush of the sea and the gentle warmth from the sun. Anna stretches out on the rocks. Their fingers touch. They lie there, together, with the tide coming in.

Black Gull Beach

Ellen Hardy

Do you remember the swarm? It happened one overheated spring when the children were going down to the beach almost every day, a cluster of them waxing and waning on the sand from mid-morning until dusk. This was on the north-west coast, safely away from the town harbour; no danger of the girls hitching lifts on motorboats bound for the mainland, or the boys turning to petty crime in the aisles of the local Spar. Their parents were happy enough to see them go, blown seawards without a thought in the hours between chores and meals. Let them enjoy it, they said. The air had a soporific note to it that spring, so that even the grown women of the island took a moment in their routines to watch the warm wind nosing past pale anemones in the uncut grass, and the men found time to stand in their quiet homes – the children being on the shore – and consider the quality of the light and shadow making strange landscapes of their familiar upholstered chairs, and picture frames, and small ornaments.

Philip McGarry was there at the lip of the sea, and Elsie Hunter, sometimes the James twins. Usually Craig Finlay.

Alex Broad, Sophie Winterson, Tara May, several others. It was a compelling place for restless children, its shifting bands of sand and grit mined with the sea's suggestive erosions and haunted by knife-sharp skeletons of petrified kelp. Peter Murray was there sometimes, too. He matched the others in age, being around ten or eleven, but his family were new to the island and he had only started at the local school the previous autumn. A slight, shy boy, with a long fringe of very fine dark hair falling into his eyes, he was merely tolerated. In football games he was always stuck in goal, and when the group scavenged driftwood for a late-afternoon bonfire he could only hang back watching crabs char in the distant flames, odd concentrations of light.

On the beach Peter too often felt a frightened muscle flicker in his jaw and would dip his head self-consciously towards his shoulder. Walking home through the fields at the end of the day he felt giddy with relief, and grateful to the cattle who returned his hopeful gaze instead of glancing down and turning away. Still he was drawn again and again to the children on the shore; each day he imagined he would discover exactly what it was they wanted in order to accept him. But he was easily distracted. His family had lived in a city in the middle of the mainland, and casual proximity to the island's wildlife amazed him. Transfixed by the massive proportions and precisely marked feathers of gulls bickering over nearby rubbish, he would miss the football pelting past him and earn a rigid silence from his team. When the children strung out along the waterline and competed at skimming stones, he abandoned the game at the sight of a grey seal keeping watch from the waves. Lingering over its dappled curves and the huffing sound of its curious breath over the water, he was alarmed to feel a hot accumulation of blood in the front of his shorts and had to crouch down and start to dig through the crisp shingle at the edge of the sea, pretending to look for shells.

Peter was one of the first there on the day of the swarm. He had squabbled with his younger sister, Clara, at breakfast – a tense and pointless dispute ending in tears and a milky mess of spilled Weetabix. He left the house bent into an ache of injustice, dwelling viciously on the way the skin on Clara's neck rolled with excess fat, and how the placement of a mole on her cheek always made her seem as if she had overlooked a blot of mud or ink. He didn't expect the other children to be at the shore so early, and was glad of it. He saw himself finding a salt-bleached branch and pacing dramatically up and down the empty sands, swiping at the breaking waves, until he felt better. Jogging up the final incline of the dunes before coming in sight of the sea he felt superior and self-consciously adult in his solitude. At first he thought the shore's appearance was a trick of the light, or that the spring tides had shifted it altogether, reconfiguring the known contours of stone and sand. But quickly his brain caught up and he understood that the beach was almost entirely covered in jellyfish.

The scale of the swarm and its extent bewildered him. It reached inland what seemed at least a hundred metres and extended patchily along the shoreline another two hundred, from where he stood to the rocks that marked the end of this part of the coast, the part known as Black Gull Beach. It looked as if it might try to breathe on its own, a partial autopsy of some giant deflated lung. It was only ten in the morning but sweat pricked along his hairline and upper lip. Perhaps the unnatural April heat was mirrored in the sea currents, he thought, imagining the jellyfish gathering and multiplying in a blood-warm slipstream before the tides deposited them in disgust at the unfamiliar invasion. He walked slowly down from the dunes towards the flat, glistening spillage. Spread out on land like this the animals were no longer floating individuals but a *thing*, a unified unintelligence. He reached the outer edge of the *thing* and crouched down to observe its constituent parts; two distinct varieties of jellyfish stirred together on the sand. One of them was smaller and more numerous, translucent, with a taut, domed body that poked up like a filled blister wherever one lay. The bell of each was thickly veined with purple, its base ringed with a gelatinous ruff of squat, violet tentacles. Below this trailed two long, elaborately frilled purple arms of almost two metres, now limply pooled into ribboned tangles. The other variety was much larger and less clearly delineated, resembling a muddle of broken eggs; it had a flattish, roundish shape with a snotlike blur of orange at the centre, falling loosely away to a frayed mess of pale flaccid tubes. There were thousands of both of them on the beach, and they were by and large still alive.

'Jesus Christ.' A voice: it was as if Peter had been drifting alone on a raft at sea and a figure had stepped out from behind a wave. Big, red-headed Craig Finlay with a sunburnt face and a football under his arm had nothing to do with this weird extravagance. Craig didn't sound shocked, he was making a statement. Peter stood and turned to him, questioning. 'Got here a while ago. Been over the rocks to see how far it goes. But it's only this bit. You didn't even hear me coming.' Peter gestured mutely at the mass of orange and purple, the bells of the domed jellyfish crinkling like popped bubble wrap under the hot salt wind. 'It's fucked up,' agreed Craig, friendlier than he had ever been before now they were alone with this mystery. 'Biblical,' he added with relish, and gobbed richly onto the nearest body. Peter wanted to investigate the swarm more closely but Craig loomed in front of him, an invitation to finally make friends. 'D'you think they're dangerous?' he asked him. Craig considered, and Peter saw that his eyes were set too close together, something he'd never noticed from a respectful distance. 'Nah,' decided Craig. 'We're too far north, won't do us much damage. Though these days, who knows,' he concluded, gesturing knowingly at the overbright sky. At close quarters he smelled of rotting sweat and Monster Munch, and he held no appeal. Peter nudged at the seeping edges of the mass with the plastic toe of his canvas shoe. The creatures were surprisingly firm, more like rubber than jelly, and he extended a foot and tested their collective surface while Craig looked on interestedly. 'G'wan my son,' he urged genially, showing no inclination to follow. With both his feet placed on the back of the thing Peter entered a new dimension, alone with the swarm and its slow, enormous thoughts. Salt water and tentacles soaked his shoes, soon followed by a dull tingling that must have been the dying beasts' mild poison. He took another step forward, then another.

Many years later, when his marriage was failing, Peter would try to remember the calm he felt as he made his way across the jellyfish. The morning sun reflecting off their surface created a blinding band of light that split his view of sea, land and sky into jagged fragments. His steps were uncertain but he felt a form of perfect control somehow related to the strangeness of his environment, as if he were underwater but held safe by a mask and breathing apparatus. He kept going

151

until he was roughly at the centre of the swarm, as far from a clear stretch of beach and the sea as possible. Then he looked down at his feet, squelching into the viscous blanket. He crouched carefully down and extended a fingertip to one of the clear inflated domes, testing its give. He found it wasn't as it appeared, an empty air sac, but filled with solid glutinous tissue. A penknife from his trouser pocket only indented the surface with a first tentative prod, but he insisted. The blade snicked satisfyingly through the jelly flesh, segmenting it along the violet veining so it opened out like a jungle flower. Then he started paring it away into translucent slivers, amazed at the texture of his material. He went more carefully near the tentacles, but managed to saw through the base of the animal so that it tore fully apart, revealing the soft, folded intricacies of its boneless interior. He speared the sagging corpse and lifted it to his nose, sniffing, but caught only sand and salt water. For the other jellyfish, the eggy one, he pulled out a lighter. He used the knife to upend the specimen nearest him, exposing its furled, soggy underbelly in a hopeless heap. Setting the lighter to the yellowish lump, he watched the tentacles start to blacken and crimp under the small flame, and smiled.

Sounds filtered in from beyond his lone dimension. The other children had started to arrive, gasping and screaming as they crested the dunes and came in sight of the swarm. Peter stood and watched them gather along the border of his domain. They weren't paying him any attention – he had misstepped again, making a gesture too bold, too solitary for admiration. He watched them poke at the edges of the thing with sticks, ignorant of his dazzling and intricate knowledge of its most intimate parts. Everyone was there now – Sophie Winterson,

Philip McGarry, Tara May and the rest. Clumsily, they were also beginning to investigate the material possibilities of the thing – jellyfish lifted and speared and used as weapons, Philip McGarry chasing Tara May screeching into the surf. But grown-ups were there now too, crying *Good lord, never seen anything like it, Stop it, Philip, that's cruel, Come back here, What on earth is that boy doing out there? What's his name? Peter? PETER!* Peter breathed for a moment longer the private air of his sanctuary, the vanquished specimens lying eviscerated at his feet. He watched the distant human figures bunch and split, together and apart, ignoring their wild gestures, and was pleased to observe Craig Finlay putting a jellyfish down Elsie Hunter's T-shirt.

A decade unfolded, then another. The swarm was largely forgotten, though people would still sometimes ask 'Do you remember . . . ?' Curling newspaper clippings remained pinned to a board in the town library. While warm springs were no longer a matter for comment, jellyfish swarms of the scale they remembered had not been reported. Somewhere along the line Peter married Elsie Hunter and settled on the island for good, finding a decent job in the planning office. This surprised his family, who moved back to the mainland once his sister Clara had finished school – it had been an adventure while the children were still young, but not for ever. Peter could tell they felt responsible, as if his decision to stay – which, though they never said it, he knew they saw as parochial – was somehow their fault. He could never explain to them the sense of possibility he felt on the island and nowhere else, that one day he might turn a corner and find the familiar made iridescent and anew. When he and

Elsie divorced he felt cheated, as if a magician had promised him a white rabbit but rummaged in his top hat and pulled out only handfuls of bedding straw. Once the paperwork was finalised he took to walking long looping circuits around the island in his free time, preferring to be on the move, finding that he thought of little as long as he kept his eyes trained on the horizon where sea met sky. When he did think of Elsie it was most often as he had imagined her when threatened with sexual failure: the curve of her hip bloomed to a seal's fatness, her skin thickened and spread with the close-set fur of a white pup. It was an image that had sustained him through nights of anxiety, of drunkenness, and for a time through her increasing disappointment and eventual scorn.

His walks rarely took him to Black Gull Beach, but leaving his office in town one day in early autumn, something about the schoolchildren with their new-term satchels made him turn his steps towards the north-western edge of the island. He passed new developments of bungalows whose construction he'd helped approve, the humming wind farm, fields scattered with fat sheep like dabs of butter. Coming onto the beach from the coast path that brought him level with the rocks at its most southern point he felt suddenly bereft, though he hadn't consciously been harbouring expectations. The beach was empty, its brightness swirled with the oncoming colours of autumn, yellow and blue blending to grey. He slowed his pace and tracked across it, kicking at the high-tide line of seaweed hopping with sandflies, chunks of old furniture, sea-frayed specimens of fifty different needless human uses for plastic. Six-pack yokes, tampon applicators, limbless dolls, sandwich packaging, dental picks. Life's ins and outs shaped into gobbets of polyethylene, doubling as ball gags for any passing sea otter or guillemot. He was almost on top of the seal before he realised that it was an animal, rather than a sad collapse of tarpaulin or pile of driftwood. It lay quietly with the rest of the detritus, and did not resist his approach. He thought perhaps it was dead, but the eye nearest him followed him as he came closer. It was surprisingly small; he'd read somewhere that their size had diminished in recent years. It was also sick, its hide darkened and its head and flippers rimmed by an oily sheen. He traced its immobility to a noose of blue plastic rope that had tightened and chafed just above the tail. The skin had been rubbed pink and raw and was now infected, a suppurating gangrenous ring that must have been poisoning the creature's blood for some time.

Peter was able to walk right up to it. He found it repulsive. A sickening smell hung around its body and flies gathered along the edges of the wound. He straightened up and looked around, as if Craig Finlay might appear and tell him what to do. But Craig had left the island years before for a shiny job running ad campaigns in America; Peter was alone with the greying beach and the dying seal. He stood and watched it; it seemed to look straight back at him without fear. The image returned of the desiccated jellyfish, his strange morning's work twenty years before, and for a wild moment he imagined the seal was challenging him to dissect it, too, or to perform some other abomination, dragging it like Hector across the beach by its rope. He also thought of rescue, or mercy: cutting its throat, calling a sanctuary or a vet. But he didn't lift his hand to find his phone in his pocket; he stood and held the seal's gaze, allowing the look to extend between them. As he continued to stare, he thought of the time when he was a teenager and his grandfather died – a man he barely knew, so he remembered it not for the experience of loss but for the memory of his father, who on the morning of the news was not visibly distressed but somehow agitated, never quite coming to rest as he moved through the house, while Peter's mother sat quite still and waited for it to be over. Eventually his father placed his hands on the kitchen sink – it looked out over the back garden, but Peter was quite sure his father wasn't seeing the unkempt square of grass with its low stone wall and the fields beyond – and said as he might of a successful shopping trip or a completed tax return, 'Well, that's it then.' The same words, Peter now realised, he had said to Elsie when she finally appeared with a suitcase. Even at the time he had delivered them with a sense of irony, though she hadn't noticed and he hadn't been sure why the moment felt so familiar.

The seal's eyes were closed, and Peter could no longer remember what he was doing there, or why it mattered. He turned and walked back in the direction of the harbour, leaving the animal where it lay.

Olive and Red

Kerry Hood

Olive and Red live on Overcliff Road in the end bungalow opposite the Zig that zags down to the beach. If you look out of their window and close one eye you can follow the laser line scoring the horizon and see boats racing from the Isle of Wight to Old Harry Rocks. Go out of their gate and over the road and you can point your binoculars at a black spot in the sky and track a squall coming in from the west and guess which useless wave the surfers will try to ride and watch it all from the calming grasses of the clifftop where you can sit on a rotten bench and fall head-first to your death.

Olive and Red, inside.
The Rover extinct in the garage. But this is nice, look: the curtains open, a spring morning, and coming under the door, the mashed green of first-cut lawns but not a puff of brack off the sea.

Olive and Red, in the front room.
Sitting on paisley armchairs rollered with grime. Leaflets

157

carding out across the low table. Underneath, tiny cones of wood being mined by things alive still. Olive suddenly fancies a magazine, one of those with double-page close-ups of golden handbags and a free squeezy pillow of face cream. She'd have to find enough change – his 'pocket money' they call it – and he wouldn't know which one to buy. And so.

Olive, not hearing the sea.

Triple-glazed windows, vibrating in the wake of an open-top bus. Olive looks up, out. Red looks up, out. Something ricochets down the chimney – a bird egg a snail a baby something pushed to its death. Olive jerks and turns to the galaxy of mould on the white frames. On the sill: circles and rectangles in dust, left by what displayed themselves there. She thinks of that toy where you have to find the right shape to fill the right space and you know they've made a space for every shape – a shape for every space no shape left behind no space forever black air – so it's daft to panic. She looks down, bends her feet. It's a beautiful little house, for a family.

'Red, I have itchy feet.'

'"No. Job. Too. Small",' he reads. 'The "too" is a number, look. "No job 2 small".'

'How funny, that.'

'It *is* funny, Olive. Now, be good while I get the Nescaff on.'

Olive, at the window.

Perched like a dog on the rim of a high-back. Her coffee is cold. When passers-by glide along the low wall her spine stretches, her nostrils do a bit of a whistle. Red comes, puts freckle fists fat onto the sill and looks across the road to the rotten bench and back into the window and Olive's reflection: her small face, its long nose with the hill in the middle, the slump of her neck when each person has passed, this small face taking all his view. She's sitting forward now, smiling on the edge of the chair as though she's waiting for this wonderful *thing* to happen.

'Wife,' he says. 'Come.'

Olive and Red, in the front garden.
Sitting on laddering canvas under yellow-belly cloud behind the trellis and dry snake of last year's climber. 'You warm enough, Olive? There's a chill.'

'Yes, love, there *is* a chill, but shut your eyes and pretend yourself warm.'

Red, after bringing out the leaflets.
He reads. Olive doesn't. There's an operation she could have that would let her read again but she has this chest. And so. It's always this. But today, outdoors, it's a different kind of waiting. Now and then Red reads something in a funny voice that mocks her hazy northern one: '"Say Goodbye To Erectile Disappointments!"' She smiles, can't laugh with this chest. 'But Olive, I mean, look at this, shoving erectile disappointments through a person's letterbox.'

Red, without a rise, falls. Sometimes their arms faint over the deckchairs, they lock little fingers, fill the space with a bridge of sighs. He tries a signed commentary on the passers-by, charades about their cagoules or bald heads or gabble voices. Olive doesn't know what he's doing but nods and laughs and coughs and gorges the air and Red is silent. A car goes along the Overcliff with its radio up and windows down and oh perhaps a girl and a boy in the back kissing, the girl with black hair and cherry earrings and first denim shorts cutting her in half and Olive feels everything starting up over the low wall and suddenly her stomach mines into her nerves, alive still, and she's fighting to remember what it is that's scratching at her throat, knowing only that she misses that thing, that bareness in her feet on the prom . . .

. . . with the hut at our backs and the shush and shing of the waves and then here they come, the splashes and shloops of my girl down there on the shore, her red feathers flying her pals running after her like chicks and the tuts from the next hut about the joy in the crops of these children and then my girl hopping up the sea wall, talons round my arm, 'We're hungry Mum we're starving' and the Calor-gas bacon sponging its Mother's Pride Thick Sliced and the hot chocolate turning tongues to fire until slow talk of their dives and lies about sharks nudging their thighs and all of it to have the next day sitting seaward, watching my girl on the shore with her heels in yesterday's sand, with the sun just up, hair bleeding still in the rise. Rose. *Rose*, that's it.

Olive, thinking about the beach hut.

'I was thinking about the beach hut.'

'We had to give it up, Olive.'

'Why did we?'

'It wasn't my fault, it was the rates, them crooks up the Town Hall.'

Olive hears her everyday wheeze but right now there's something on top, a beat pressing into her obstacle airway, a scratch carving the named thing. Stop. 'Still, this is nice, love.'

'If you're happy, I'm happy,' Red says. 'What else d'you want to know?'

He gives the back of her hand a peck and Olive's beat burns out. She looks towards the Zig, running down it with her black eyes but she has these feet and this chest, and so. Only, her hands, they are balling, pulsing now at the knuckles, fists pushing along her dress, her eyes running down the Zig right-left-right like a bee finding its fix, Olive running and darting and starting to rise but Red suddenly battens down his Velcro loafers and walks out of the gate.

Olive squints at his stubby body moving along the wall. His fringe of white hair with the finger of fire still in it. There's a slash in her throat, pulling itself apart, sending a pin up through her face to find the thing to remember, to bring it into her voice and out. She slaps the canvas, ring finger catching on the frame, sending a shock up to her elbow. She can't get up, not at all. While Red disappears along Overcliff Road, Olive's spine slides her down the deckchair until she's below the sand, scraping against bones of slaves and crusts of dinosaurs and petrified pines and veins of bronze and iron and the vanished land that was once joined with France – all life thought to be extinguished but really preserved in salt and rock, and waiting.

Everyone, trying to remember everything.
It's daft to panic, she knows. And what if it isn't just me? What if it's everyone, trying to remember everything? Or trying not to remember, trying to get under the rocks, trying to come out new, scrubbed like a pumice bath and able to do everything right and able to breathe.

Red and his mysterious walks.

It's the family joke. Like Olive and Red – never just Olive, never just Red – Olive and Red Olive-and-Red. Now Olive wheezes with the need suddenly to know where he walks. Does he have a woman? Perhaps she's called . . . *Lena*, yes, *Lena* gives him swimming lessons because he's afraid of water but with *Lena* he lifts off the tiles. Or this woman has no name but hair all over her body and they sit in her conservatory while he shaves her onto a tarpaulin.

Red rolls a wheelbarrow through the gate. Hauls Olive up. Tips bags of sand across the pebbles, sets the deckchairs on top and opens his arms, the magic performed.

'Where's all this from?'

'It was there, Olive, on the driveway.'

'Not our driveway though.'

'Not ours, no.'

Olive's throat stings but she pushes herself upright because of the sun coming and the lovely sand, and she shuffles indoors for ice cream, a sound at her shoulder blades like a twin, gasping.

Olive and Red, stabbing at plastic tubs with teaspoons.

'It's an unusual taste, Olive.'

'What have I written on the side?'

'"Butter. Bean. Mash."'

'Oh.'

'People looked at me, with that wheelbarrow.'

'I should think so. You've got your pyjama bottoms on. With your thing out.'

Olive and Red, sucking butter bean slush.

'Oh, here's a proper flush of day – thank you, sun!' says Olive, face to the sky. She tries to kick off her shoes.

Red says, 'That singer, the one you like.'

'With the husky voice?'

'She's been on the radio.'

'I love her.'

'She's dead.'

'Oh don't tell me oh Red.'

'I'm just saying something.'

A boy and his mother, coming by.

The mother side-eyes the bungalow, not cutting her stride towards the Zig, but the boy double-takes, stops and puts both hands on the low wall. A small animal scanning for food, for predators, for others of his kind. He shakes his head trying to figure it out, this sinking house with its drive ski-sloping down to the front door and the salt-crust corrosions and weatherboard dormer and terrible tears of bird shit and dry fountain gunned with lichen and its façade cemented with half-shells from every ocean and blue glass from sailing ships and bits of marmalade pots and crab claws all fizzing out of the bungalow's guts. He can make out bits of humans too and dips along the wall to catch the whole of them. Two old people on a beach in a garden opposite a *real* beach. He leans in, thin upper body rippling over the wall –

'Get here!' (His mother.)

A head robots up: the old woman, waving out of her trellis frame. The old man is asleep or dead. The boy holds his hand high, a frozen breaker to match hers.

'Now!'

The boy runs off and is just going down the Zig when he turns and smiles and the laser line shoots into Olive and she smells at last the dewed clifftop and the nests of sand martins home from Africa and the fists of honeyed thrift and that brack off the sea and bladderwrack and furbelows and mermaid's tresses and the rust cloaking the great groynes and the gasping fish on the charters round the bay and sun oil sweating in its polythene bag and the hot chocolate and Rose's hair salting across Olive's neck and as the boy disappears she knows it isn't the beach she craves and she cries out and follows the postman into the house.

Olive and Red, in the hallway.
'They're coming for our house.'
   'They can't have the house, Olive.'
   'This letter says they can.'
   'We'll get one of them sheltered places.'
   '*This* is my sheltered place.'
   'I'll sort it out.'
   'What have you been doing?'
   'I thought I'd win us the lottery.'
   'I only wanted the beach hut.'
   'Olive.'
   'You've done it again.'
She goes to lie down in the back room and dreams of leaving.

Thieving secretive man.
In her dream she's knocking on doors with a suitcase at her beautiful toes in their pearl stilettos, all the doors on all the streets. She knocks on all the doors every time a letter comes

and every time, one door opens. Now though, not even a crack of light. All the doors are shut. She wakes, sore feet brimming over each other and lets herself remember all of it now, though she can hardly swallow with a half-century of thistles in her throat. The letters over the years, hundreds of letters, hidden or torn to bits or shoved up the chimney or posted under the car mat, driver's side. Cheque stubs left blank. Jumping up for the phone and saying 'Wrong number.' Thieving secretive man waiting to intercept the postman. Bills in her name still getting through for credit cards she doesn't have, bailiffs at the door, not knowing why, Red saying nothing. Olive paying them off, going with grown-up Rose to the bank and sliding off a chair in the manager's office because there were no savings 'just a lot of things your husband must settle, or maybe you'd prefer to call the police?' She thought he was done with all that, whatever 'that' was. Now they're coming for the house.

Forgiving forgiving forgiving.

Olive and the racket.

She gets up because of the racket and goes to the front room. There's sand wall to wall, deep enough for swishing ankles. There's a shovel and the stolen wheelbarrow. There's Red, tributaries of sweat rafting his thieving secretive stubble, shush and shing nudging the hinges of the open door as he takes her hands in his hot fists and walks backwards, guiding her along the shore and into the deckchair.

'Nearly killed me, Olive. Up and down the Zig with that wheelbarrow.'

She looks up at him. His mouth skids over her cheek. The door is still open.

'My trouble is,' she says, 'I just love life.'

Olive and Red, in the afternoon light on an island of sand.
Happy and smiling in glassy pools of themselves. So that when
the football comes pouring down the drive and through the
open door and the boy runs in after it, his breath is taken. His
mother follows. She wide-eyes the sand and ebbs one foot out
of the door, rubbing a mark off her gold sliders because today
she's Dettol'd everything including the boy in his three-quarter
khakis and yellow hoodie. Olive recognises this boy as the first
to wave back and knows straightaway that despite his surfy
clothes he's never been in the sea and that however old he is, he
looks younger. He sees this old woman doing a half-cock smile
then nodding at the sand. He looks at his mother who wrings
her lips. It's her code for fun and he knows that inside her
bowl of cheeks it's waiting to burst out, that a big fat laugh
is coming. She does it when she sees twins and three-legged
dogs and other things she's scared of and now her eyebrows
are going up which means the game is on. He tries to join in.

Only, he sees the belly ring pushing at her top, the skinny
jeans, and for the first time sees the weld of his mother there
and has to look away and even though this day is supposed to
be about him and her, he looks instead at the old lady: goat-
horn toes, grated shin skin, oaty forearms, ring with Sellotape
over, a dinner-splash dress and these chest tags like footholds
on a climbing wall, this neck with tea-plantation ridges
ending at a collapsed face and marble eyes and gunmetal hair.
He knows he can't play his mother's game.

'Hallo!' Red makes the boy jump. 'Have you come to
look about you?'

'Yes please.'

'Oh,' says Olive. 'You're an angel what are you?' (The
boy stares.) 'You're an angel, that's what.'

The boy blinks up and down this ancient sea creature. Red looks at the football. The boy throws it, Red heads it behind, the mother shouts 'Enough!' and the boy stands rigid though there's nothing to hit. The room is empty apart from dirty chairs, table, bookshelf, a ginger girl framed on the mantelpiece, invisible pictures on the wall and these deckchairs sinking into the sand. Even so, the mother pulls him towards her so hard that he spins off both legs. 'You *don't* go into people's houses they could be psychos or make you itch and how would you like it if people just walked into ours?'

The boy opens his mouth but sits at the old couple's feet. Nothing happens but he *expects*.

Eventually Olive says, 'Will you have ice cream, angel?' Red leaps up. The mother stares at his pyjama bottoms. Olive says, 'He had his thing out before.'

'No thanks,' the mother says. 'We're allergic.'

'To butter beans?'

'And we got to go. My feet are freezing me.'

'Wait till you've got these feet, love.'

'No thanks I'm not getting old, I'll shoot myself and I'm not even being horrible.' She cocks her ear towards the door. The boy starts to rise.

'Show him your Indian!' Red says. The boy, caught between getting up and cross-legging down, falls flat on his face. He's up immediately, doing an exaggerated metronome creep and finds himself at the bookshelf with *The Wondrous World of Stories for* . . . (here, the spine is torn).

'We got to go. Run out of foil. For the windows.'

Olive takes a photo from her purse and Red hands it to the mother. 'She sends money and gets a picture to put in her

167

handbag.'

'Lovely isn't she?' Olive says. '*Anita*.'

'What's wrong with her?' the mother asks.

'She's just poor, love.'

The mother passes the photo to the boy and says, 'I'm not being horrible, but.' The boy studies it, gives it to Olive and looks into her and nods. She puts a finger on the tip of his nose.

'You should have seen my wife at your age,' Red says to the mother who's scuffing at the sand. 'The image of Ingrid Bergman.'

The mother stops. Scans the blinking grains. Lets out a breath that she doesn't know about. Draws a slow half-circle with her foot. 'So you two, you're like a tourist attraction?'

Olive smiles. 'No, love, we're just us and we have a daughter, Rose.'

Red says, 'She lives in London.'

'Yes, we went once, Red drove, it was lovely.'

'And where do you live?' Red asks the boy.

'Up the Flats.'

'The old water tower? What a place to live!'

'Why?'

'You can keep watch for invaders.'

'What's "invaders"?'

'Vikings for a start.'

'What about zombies?'

'Especially zombies, they're right buggers.'

'Have you seen one?'

'Oh they don't bother with bungalows. But a water tower, that's the place!' The mother is spinning her key ring. Red catches her eye. 'That singer's been on, with the throaty voice.'

'I hate her,' she says.

'She's dead.'

'Don't look at me, I didn't kill her. Sorry, fuck. Sorry.' (To the boy:) 'We got to get going.'

Olive, though, wanders off, the boy following as she whispers, 'Now, angel, what can I give you?'

Something falling, down the chimney.

The boy jumps, moves closer to Olive, twists his fingers. Her hand lands on his shoulder. He steps forward, wants to bury himself against her and he doesn't like it and so he concentrates on the pig curl of hair at her chin that he hopes his mother doesn't see and he mimes, I Just Heard Something.

Yes, Angel, That's The Salt People.

But They're Running Down The Chimney.

They Have Strong Legs. I Can't Go Up Chimneys With These Feet.

My Sister Can't Go Out. We Have To Shut The Curtains. She's Allergic.

We Like The Curtains Shut Too. Bring Your Sister For A Play.

I Can Still Hear Them.

Call Up. Go On, Love.

What Do I Say?

Ask Them To Come And Play.

What Do I Play?

He peers up the chimney, cold air arrowing his eyeballs. He sees them suddenly, the salt people, their coal-blackness, their crystal feet running-stopping-running, their eyes flashing, it makes him scared and excited. Olive touches the back of his hair then her own arms, too soft now for holding a child high on the hip. She tries to give him *The Wondrous World of Stories for Girls*. He shakes his head. He doesn't get given things. He's never had grandparents. He's never been in a bungalow. Maybe all old people give you girls' books and have beaches in their front rooms. Still, he wants the old woman to keep standing next to him even though she smells of something wrong. His mother is saying his name and Olive says, 'We'll see you again' but he wonders how, as it's been an accidental visit. She starts to shrink, the man, too, with his old elbows on his knees. The boy drops down, starts egg-timing the sand through his fingers. His mother goes across. In one movement her hand shoots out, roughs his hair, smooths it. She smiles and he's back four years ago, her looking through the Infants' railings blowing kisses as he waits to be paired up for the first time, him turning away just as she's wiping a sleeve across her face.

Something Olive remembers.
'You're Tanika's daughter. Tanika was in the Juniors when I was doing the dinners. Oh she turned out lovely. She used to go past here and wave in. Always pushing you up and down that Zig.'

'I don't even see her now, so.'

A silence while everyone but Olive runs away. 'He'll be all right for a bit, love,' she says. The mother flicks one of her tangerine nails with another. 'Right, Trouble,' she says to the boy. 'I'm getting the foil and I want you outside here in one hour.' She goes past Red and nods and says, 'I don't know who Ingrid Bergman is.'

Olive leads her out and leans against the front door.

'You've such a pretty face. I've run out of lippy.'

'It's all fucked up today. You've been nice though. Later then.'

Olive calls, 'I don't want to be Ingrid Bergman. I want him to be Cary Grant.'

The boy, crawling over the sand to the kitchen.
Banging cupboard doors. Returning with equipment. Keeping his eyes off the chimney, sitting, spreading vessels, beginning. He levels the dunes, packs sand into saucepans and Tupperware, planing the tops with the precision of a woodworker. Counts one-two-three, upends a pan and pummels it with a spatula before lifting it away and placing little tipped pots on top. Shapes the moat then goes to the garden, bringing back shells to shore up the walls of a channel that starts to loop its way to the hall. Olive and Red make oohs and aahs, the boy busy and silent and admired. At last he leans back on his heels. Olive and Red applaud.

'Oh, angel!'

'Extraordinary!'

The boy bites his lip. 'It's a castle.'

'With a lighthouse!' Red says. 'It just needs a flash.'

'What's a lighthouse?'

Red and the boy, making the lighthouse flash.
The hour is up. Red says to keep the torch. The boy says, 'I'll see you again' and the old man says, 'Yes, when you're needing to look about you.'

Olive opens and closes her mouth. The boy waves and says, 'I'm an angel what am I?'

The boy has gone.

Olive is having a little cry. Red is looking for her inhaler. Neither of them sees the tangerine nails poking through the letterbox, a rose lipstick dropping onto the mat.

Olive and Red, in the darkening front room.
There's an empty bottle. Flat lemonade in mugs, no boy, a Dairylea flag on the castle. Here's Red, boarding up the windows from the inside to make a beach hut.

'They can't have the house, Olive.'

Something bulges in from outside but they are safe. Olive's beat has stopped for she knows that nothing getting thrown down the chimney can come in. Red has stopped up the stack, Red has stilled the air, Red has seen off all invaders. Olive is coughing for England but this is nice, look, this horizontal slat staying off to see the last of the sun. And so.

'Red.'

'Olive?'

'Rose called you "Father". Never "Dad".'

'I liked it. It was dignified.'

'You twitched whenever she said it.'

'Olive.'

'Like a dog being slapped on the nose.'

'Olive.'

'She stopped calling you Dad when she found the word "torturer". You were torturing us, she said, by never saying what you'd done, making us not know. Tell me now, what you've done with it, that little egg of money I started the day we came south. That little egg I've waited a half-century to crack.' Silence. 'Tell me, Red, why I've cleaned other people's toilets, fed other people's children, typed other people's wills, tried losing my accent, stuck with you for our Rose who doesn't even want to know us. All I wanted was this little house up here and the beach hut down there with waves and children and the sea on my legs and air in my lungs and the sun and a fat moon on the water and our girl coming to visit with her own little ones but she doesn't come and there'll be no house for her. Look around us, we've nothing, so where's it all gone oh you've that face on, what have we to do Red tell me what we've to do oh don't cry ignore me love I'm queer today I'm loop-the-loop.'

'Here's your whiffer.'

'It's no wonder I'm wheezy.'

'Olive.'

'I've been holding my breath for years.'

'Olive.'

'Red?'

'You're my everything you are.'

Olive and Red, asleep or something else.

A gleam. The boy, leading his mates to the window. They peer in at the slit, hardly able to see the sand and the deck-chair creatures, but pay their bets anyway and run off while the boy comes in and shines his lighthouse lamp at the lip-stick then into the old man's face – asleep or something else – then up the chimney, first kicking in the cardboard and jumping back at the scatterings, the remains of the salt people crusting his shoes. He turns to the window and pulls at a slat then at another until the last one splits, flinging him back and flattening the Dairylea flag while the sun sends its ends up the cliff into the glass and Olive and Red blink as the boy comes back breathless from the kitchen with an overflowing bucket.

Red understands and gets to work on a paper boat called *No Job 2 Small*. The boy gives Olive the lipstick. She gasps and kisses it as a wind starts to funnel its howling under the door, coming for them across their front-room beach, but she digs in her horns, looks at the angel lighting up the sand and when he dips a cup into the bucket she licks her lips and Red drops to his knees and she follows, their hands bowling water along the gutter and as the moat starts to fill, the old woman and the old man and the boy breathe faster, they're chuckling, look, and coughing a bit and discovering, as the front room floats free in its ocean, just how thirsty they have become.

Authors' Bios

Holly Barratt is from the East Midlands but lives in Cardiff. She has been making up stories since she was tiny and completed an MA in creative writing at the University of Chichester in 2007. She is currently working on a novel which, like much of her writing, is inspired by the sea.

Emily Bullock won the Bristol Short Story Prize with 'My Girl', which was broadcast on BBC Radio 4. Her stories appear in collections such as *Aesthetica Creative Writing Annual*, *A Short Affair* (Scribner), and *The Bath Short Story Award Anthology*. Her debut novel, *The Longest Flight* (Myriad), was shortlisted for the Cross Sports Book Awards, and listed in the *Independent*'s Paperbacks of the Year.

Ellen Hardy begins her PhD in creative-critical writing at the University of East Anglia in autumn 2019. Her fiction has been published or is forthcoming in *The Mechanics' Institute Review* and *A Wild and Precious Life: A Recovery Anthology*, and shortlisted for the Myriad Editions First Drafts Competition.

Rosanna Hildyard is an editor and writer from North Yorkshire. Her fiction and journalism has been published by *FlashBack Fiction, Under the Radar*, Poetry School and the *Darlington & Stockton Times*, among others. She lives in London and is working on her first novel.

Kerry Hood's awards include Words and Women Award, and Cinnamon Press and Frome Festival Short Story prizes. She was highly commended in the Costa Short Story Award and Manchester Fiction Prize and a runner-up in the Bridport Prize. Her stories are broadcast on BBC Radio 4. Plays include *Meeting Myself Coming Back* at Soho Theatre (*British Theatre Guide* Highlight, *Sunday Times* Critics' Choice, shortlisted Meyer-Whitworth Award).

Isha Karki is a writer living in London. Her short fiction has appeared in *Lightspeed Magazine, Mslexia* and *The Good Journal*, and is forthcoming in anthologies *Rosalind's Siblings* from Galli Books and *On Relationships* from 3 of Cups Press. She is a graduate of Clarion West 2019.

James Mitchell is a science fiction, magical realism and true story writer and performer from London. He graduated from the Birkbeck Creative Writing MA in 2015, and since then has spent his time trying to smuggle strange tales into places like *Vice*, *GQ*, and the fourth plinth of Trafalgar Square. @jamescmitchell

Melody Razak completed an MA in creative writing at Birkbeck three years ago with a distinction. Since then, she has been working on her first novel, *Moth*, and putting together a collection of short stories. She has been published in *The Mechanics' Institute Review* and has had a short story 'highly recommended' by the Bath Short Story Award.

T. Schroeder is a writer of prose and poetry based in England. She has published work in magazines and publications both online and in print. Her story 'And Our Land Will Yield Its Harvest' was longlisted for the Galley Beggar Short Story Prize 2017. She is working on a novel.

Toby Wallis's writing has appeared in *Glimmer Train*, *The Nottingham Review* and *Belle Ombre*, among others. He is a winner of *Glimmer Train*'s Short Story Award for New Writers, and has been shortlisted for the Bridport Prize and the Raymond Carver Short Story Contest.

Sylvia Warren is an academic editor and writer. Her fiction has been published in *Open Pen*, *Burning House Press*, and *The Island Review*. She is a contributing editor at *3:AM Magazine* and the literary features writer for *OX Magazine*. You can find her on Twitter @sylvswarren.

Judith Wilson is a London-based journalist and writer. She was shortlisted for the London Short Story Prize 2018, won first prize for the Lorian Hemingway Short Story Competition 2017, and was shortlisted for the Bath Short Story Award 2017. She is studying for the MA Creative Writing at Royal Holloway, University of London, and is writing her first novel. www.judithwilsonwrites.com

Thanks

Every writer who entered our inaugural short story competition, for their stories and for making the competition's continuation a possibility.

The twelve writers whose stories make this anthology.

Brick Lane Bookshop for funding this project and believing I could create a prize and book.

The judges: Kit Caless, Zoe Gilbert and Emma Paterson.

The first readers: Xanthi Barker, Andrew Carson, Glenn Collins, Kalina Dimitrova, Andrew Everitt, Denise Jones, Jarred McGinnis, Tom Norton, Sophia Pearson and Mazin Saleem.

Polly Jones for anonymising.

Sue Tyley for her precision copy-editing and support.

The team at Brick Lane Bookshop. For your enthusiasm for the project and support.

181

Everyone who listed or tweeted about the prize: Paul McVeigh, Aerogramme Writers' Studio, MIROnline, NAWE, *Neon*, Creative Writing Ink, Spread the Word, *Sunday Times* Short Story Award and many more.

Rosie Arrowsmith for writing an article for MIROnline.

Daniel Kramb, Lucy Norman and many others for advice and encouragement along the way. You know who you are, thank you all.